The GRAND, GENIUS Summer of HENRY HOOBLER

The GRAND, GENIUS *Summer* of HENRY HOOBLER

LISA SHANAHAN

Illustrations by Judy Watson

ALLEN&UNWIN
SYDNEY • MELBOURNE • AUCKLAND • LONDON

First published by Allen & Unwin in 2017

Allen & Unwin
83 Alexander Street
Crows Nest NSW 2065
Australia
Phone: (61 2) 8425 0100
Email: info@allenandunwin.com
Web: www.allenandunwin.com

A Cataloguing-in-Publication entry is available
from the National Library of Australia
www.trove.nla.gov.au

ISBN 978 1 76029 301 7

Teachers' notes available at allenandunwin.com

Cover and text design by Debra Billson
Set in 11.5/16 pt ITC New Baskerville Roman

This book was printed in May 2020 by Griffin Press, part of Ovato,
168 Cross Keys Road, Salisbury South, South Australia 5106, Australia

5 7 9 10 8 6 4

For Rohan

CONTENTS

LEAVING

It was nearly time to go.

Henry tweaked the blind and peered out the window. The car was at the top of the drive. The trailer was locked on. It was bulging with the tent, tarp poles, sleeping-bags, mattresses, torches, tables, chairs, boogie boards, fishing rods and every sort of ball in the universe, including totem tennis. And there was his new silver bike, hitched to the back, the front wheel whizzing.

Henry dropped the blind. He slid down between the wall and the bed. He held his breath. If he was very quiet, they might leave without him. Maybe they wouldn't even notice he wasn't there. Then he could stay at home alone and live on tinned tuna and crackers and baked beans and never have to worry a

1

single moment about bugs, spiders, snakes, stingers, blue-ringed octopi, tsunamis, sharks and a new silver bike without training wheels.

'Heno?' Dad called. 'Are you set? Are you ready? Everyone's waiting.'

If he stayed very still and they left without him, he could sleep in his bed for the whole holiday instead of on the ground, and he wouldn't have to travel for hours and hours in the car, stuck in the middle between Patch and Lulu. His big brother Patch, who didn't talk much anymore and never wanted to play Minecraft or Monopoly or dodgeball on the trampoline, but only listen to music on his phone and joggle his leg nonstop, maybe for fifteen hours straight, maybe enough to get into the *Guinness Book of Records*. And his younger sister Lulu, who only ever wanted to play dumb ponies and speak horse!

'Hey there!'

Henry's doona flew up. All the dark and warm and the smell of boy and scruffy dog went with it.

Dad bent over. 'What are you doing down there, Heno?'

'I don't know.'

'Are you stuck?'

'No.'

'Well, it's time to go, mate,' said Dad, flicking the doona back. 'We want to hit the road before the traffic gets too bad.'

2

'Maybe you could go without me?'

Dad raised an eyebrow. 'What?'

'Mrs Neale from next door could check up on me, like she does on Charlie Olson's cat.'

'Aaah, Heno, you're a little more work than a cat, mate.'

'What about Nonna?'

'She's looking after Beatle! And he's not the sort of dog to sit on her lap. He's going to take up all her energy and time.'

Henry knew this was true. Their dog Beatle was lovable and adorable and full of goodwill – licks and love – but he never did sit still. He was all fetch and drop and go and play, from the second he woke up till the second he went to bed, and even then his four legs still raced in his dreams.

'Look, Heno, you're going to love it! We're right on the water. There's a bike path bang outside the tent. There'll be scootering, skateboarding, fishing and swimming. Everyone is going to be there. The Carsons and the Barones. It'll be fun! Like Friday night tennis, only every day.'

Henry shrugged. The Hooblers, the Carsons and the Barones had played tennis on Friday nights for a long time, ever since Patch, Dylan and Jay became close friends in kindy. But Friday night tennis was not quite as much fun lately. Patch, Dylan and Jay mostly played tennis with the adults now, because they were nearly fifteen and knew how to serve and could hit the ball over the net, more often than not. No one ever wanted to play tag or hide-and-seek or spotlight anymore. Carey spent the whole time sitting sideways in the umpire chair, reading comics, while Reed bossed Henry, Lulu and Kale around the kids' court.

'Look,' said Dad. 'There's a bunch of brilliant stuff to do down there. You'll be able to go yabbying on the sandflats and see the soldier crabs marching out like a tiny blue army. And the stingrays down by the wharf, if we're lucky!' He leant his knee on the bed. 'It'll be paradise! Yelonga is my favourite place in the world. The place I camped with my family when I was a boy like you.'

Stingrays! Holy Kamoley! No one had mentioned stingrays before. What if Henry fell off the wharf and landed on top of one and it carried him out into the deep and he slipped off and ended up being swallowed by a whale shark?

'At night, we'll play board games and cards, sizzle some sausages and watch the sky light up with stars.'

Board games and cards! Henry played his Nonna every Thursday afternoon, when Patch was at soccer and Lulu was at dancing. And not just baby games like Snakes and Ladders. He was always smashing his Nonna at Monopoly and Cluedo and Up the River, Down the River, and it wasn't because she was going easy on him, either.

Dad grinned. 'And you know what, Heno, there'll be gelato! Gelato like you've never tasted. Every flavour under the sun. They make it from scratch! How about I personally promise you bucketloads of gelato?'

Gelato! Henry liked that too, even better than plain ordinary ice-cream. And bucketloads of flavours! The prospect sent a sparkle right up through the roof of his mouth.

'That's a big promise,' he said, gazing at the ceiling. He didn't want to appear too eager. There was the problem of his bike, after all, and still the possibility of bugs, spiders, snakes, stingers, blue-ringed octopi, tsunamis, sharks and stingrays and now maybe even whale sharks too.

'I'm confident I can deliver a mountain of gelato,' said Dad. 'Easy-peasy.'

Henry sniffed. 'All right, then,' he said, and he held out his hand so his dad could drag him from his hidey-hole.

It took ages to get out of the city.

'Everyone is going on holidays,' cried Lulu. She stared out at the cars, glittery and shiny, stopping and starting beside them.

'Ye-es,' said Dad. He drummed his fingers on the steering wheel.

Mum unwrapped another barley sugar. 'Everyone had the same good idea.'

'That's for sure,' said Dad, with a deep, deep sigh.

'Spotto!' Lulu tapped her pony against the window. 'Neigh! Marigold is winning. She just saw another yellow car.'

'How many yellow cars now?' asked Mum.

'Ten,' said Lulu.

'Good counting,' said Mum. 'See! You are ready for big school. Only a few more weeks now.'

'I don't want to talk about that,' said Lulu, folding her arms. 'I already told you.'

'Alright then,' said Mum. 'My lips are zipped. How many purple cars have you spotted?'

'Only two,' said Lulu. 'Poor Violet is getting grumpy.'

'Mmm,' said Mum. 'I don't think purple is the most popular colour.'

'There are more pink cars,' said Lulu. 'So Peony is happy. Very happy!'

Henry wriggled. 'How much longer?' he asked.

'Five and a half hours,' said Dad.

'Holy Shamoley,' breathed Henry.

'Five and a half hours! But you already said that before, when we just left home,' said Lulu.

'Ha!' said Dad. 'It's always five and half hours, no matter when you ask. Even when we're just five minutes away.'

'In other words, it's a long, long time yet,' said Mum. 'And you might as well have a rest, if you can.'

'But I'm not tired,' said Lulu, dancing her yellow pony along the windowsill.

But within five minutes she was fast asleep, her head nodding, her hair clinging to her sweaty forehead, her hot bare foot resting on Henry's knee. Smelly ponies avalanched out of her lap, sending up a sweet waft of strawberry, apple and musk.

Henry lifted Lulu's foot gently and placed it back near her booster seat. The problem with being in the middle was there was always someone on either side taking up just a bit extra, inching their way into his space. Henry shuffled across the seat away from Lulu and her ponies, accidentally nudging Patch, who grunted and flinched. 'Watch it!' he growled, opening his eyes to glare at Henry. Gosh, Patch was like some kind of pimply, snappy, carnivorous Venus flytrap!

A lump rose in Henry's throat. He slid his leg back and gazed out the front windscreen, at the vans and the station wagons and the four-wheel drives pulling caravans and trailers and boats slowly forwards, at a whole city out on the road, moving house for just a few weeks, pillows puffed up in rear windows like fat clouds.

'I didn't like going on holidays when I was

7

young.' Mum folded a crinkly clear barley sugar wrapper into a tiny square.

Henry stretched forward. 'What?' he said.

'I didn't like going on holidays when I was little.'

'How come?'

'I don't know,' said Mum, sliding the wrapper into a plastic-bag bin. 'Maybe some people are more homebodies at heart.'

Was Henry a homebody at heart? He wasn't sure. Perhaps he hadn't gone away enough to know yet. Staying with Grandpa and Grandma Hoobler probably wouldn't count as a real holiday, even though it was by the sea, because they'd been going there since he was a baby so it still felt like home. He didn't want to think about their last family camping trip. On a farm, by a river. The cows. The poo. The flies. The mud. The chickens. The hissing geese that kept popping up like horrible cartoon characters, when he least expected them. What if you were born a homebody? Did you stay that way forever?

'I love holidays,' said Dad, glancing over his shoulder. 'All the adventure and promise of new things to see and do! No clocks or timetables or places to be. Waking up and going to sleep with the sun. Alive to the wind and the sound of the sea. Aaaaah, so much opportunity! Kitesurfing and stand-up paddleboard riding, swimming, making castles and digging huge holes, skateboarding and jumping off the wharf. A plethora of pleasures.'

'Hmmm,' said Mum. 'Not everyone feels the same way.'

'I know,' said Dad. 'That's true.'

'When I was young and we were going on holidays, I always had this feeling just as we were about to leave,' said Mum. 'I couldn't quite put my finger on it back then, but looking back now, I think it might have been dread.'

'Dread?' said Dad. 'Really? What's to dread about an old holiday?'

'You know,' said Mum. 'What if something happened?'

Dad fiddled with his headrest. 'Well, you'd hope so! You'd want something to happen. No one loves a nothing sort of holiday.'

'But maybe something bad!'

Dad shook his head. 'Something bad? Geez.'

'Did something bad ever happen?' asked Henry.

'Well, no. Nothing exceptionally bad,' said Mum. 'Just the usual kinds of bad like fighting with my sisters, getting sunburnt and dumped by a big wave, dropping an ice-cream cone on the footpath before I'd even taken a lick. But even so, every time I went away, I just had this nagging worry in my chest, like a moth buzzing up against a bright porch light, that something terrible *might* happen.'

Henry nodded. He knew about that moth.

It was fluttering in his chest even now. 'Do you still get that worry?' he asked.

'Sometimes, yes,' said Mum, nodding. 'Yes. I do. It's a lot smaller now but maybe it's still there, just a little bit.'

'What do you do about it?' asked Henry.

'Oh, well,' said Mum, swivelling round, 'I don't know. I think I just notice it and even make a little room for it. Maybe I even say, *Ah, there you are!* But I also remind myself that it's not the *whole* story. That I've had very enjoyable holidays in the past and this one will likely be the same.' She smiled and the wrinkles around her eyes fanned out.

'Uh-huh,' said Henry. 'Okay. Right.' The fluttery worry was suddenly still. He tapped his fingers against his chest and breathed in deeply. His mum turned back and dug out another barley sugar from the glove box.

'Lolly, anyone?'

'No, thanks,' said Dad.

'Yes, thanks,' said Henry. His mum tossed it and he caught it first go. He snuck a sideways, hopeful glance. Ah gosh, Patch was asleep.

Henry opened the barley sugar slowly and popped it into his mouth. Before long, the edges of the lolly began to splinter. He pondered what his mum had said about making a little room for the worry. He imagined what it might look like. He was

10

pretty sure if he had to draw it, it would be a big round grey tumbleweed of dust, with skinny black-and-white-striped legs poking out and red boots, with untied shoelaces. 'Have a seat!' Henry imagined himself saying to it, plumping up a cushion. 'Would you like a glass of water?' The idea made him want to laugh out loud.

Henry gazed at his mum. She was chomping on her barley sugar. It sounded like a cliff crashing inside her mouth. She wasn't good at lolly-sucking competitions. She didn't really have the patience. Henry was always winning those competitions. He was good at holding a lolly in his mouth until it was just a sliver.

His mum wasn't so good at making cakes and slices for fundraising days either. Or remembering school notes. But she was good at knowing things. Yes, his mum was good at knowing things inside him that he didn't even have words for yet. There was something reassuring about that, like he was a trapeze artist in a circus, swinging through the sky, with the biggest, strongest safety net in the whole universe stretched out wide to catch him.

Henry crunched the last tiny sliver of barley sugar. He slid his head against the edge of Lulu's rock hard booster seat, found one tiny comfy spot and went off to sleep.

ARRIVING

And then before Henry knew it, they were nearly there.

'Woo-hooo!' cried Dad. 'Wakey-wakey, sleepyheads!'

Lulu woke with a start, her cheek damp with dribble. 'How much longer?'

'Five and a half hours,' said Dad, with a laugh.

Mum turned her head. 'Five minutes.'

Lulu pressed the button for her window. A breeze rushed in and her hair whirled about. Bellbirds pinged in the forest above them. 'I can smell sea!' she called, wiping her cheek.

Patch pushed the button for his window too. He leant his head out, his fringe lifting up like a salute. He sniffed. 'I think you're right,' he said to Lulu.

And then, after they chugged up one last hill and around a bend, they could see it. Yelonga Inlet stretched out before them. Henry let out a slow, wonderstruck breath. There were more shades of blue than he could possibly count. Patches of turquoise. Splashes of kingfisher blue. Pools of sapphire, indigo and even navy.

'Here comes the bridge,' said Dad. Their car shuddered across, the trailer jolting behind them.

'Is it a lifting bridge, Daddy?' Lulu slid forward and gazed up.

'It sure is,' said Dad, glancing out at the water. 'But the bridge only goes up when there's a big boat wanting to get in or out. Ah, what a shame, low tide! I was hoping the water would be rushing in to greet us.' He laughed. 'I thought I'd get a kitesurf out front before dark.' He turned to wink at Henry. 'But maybe I'll have to settle for a bike ride instead?'

A shivery jolt ran up Henry's spine.

'Ha-ha,' said Mum. 'Fat chance! We're going to be too busy for that.'

Thank heavens! Henry rested his head and breathed out slowly.

'Neigh!' Lulu lifted Violet, Peony and Marigold to the window. 'Neeeeigggh!' Her hair whipped about, the tips flicking into Henry's eyes.

They drove slowly up the main street, past the baker, the butcher, the chemist and supermarket, past the gelato shop with its red and white stripey awning and its long, long line of people out the front. They turned left, bouncing over a speed hump, past a sign with flashy bright letters saying *Yelonga Inlet Haven.*

'*Welcome,*' said Henry, reading the small line beneath the big letters on the sign. '*You'll Always Belonga in Yelonga!*'

'Aw, dog-goggles,' said Patch. 'Don't tell me some crazy dad-joke maniac runs this caravan park?'

'Who knows,' said Dad, pulling up outside a squat red-roofed building. 'But I'll let you in on a secret, Patch. Crazy dad-joke maniacs are everywhere. They're irrepressible, like cockroaches. You will never be rid of them.'

Patch groaned. 'Spare me, puppetino!'

'Wait here,' said Mum, opening her car door, 'while we go and book in at reception. We'll only be a second.'

Henry gazed at a whiteboard hanging up near the entrance. It was advertising a fishing charter trip out to the reef, the times for low and high tide, and the temperature of the water.

Lulu unclicked her seatbelt, scooped up her ponies and clambered across Henry to sit in Patch's lap. 'Watch what you're doing, dingbat,' grunted Henry, flapping his hand at her legs.

Lulu poked out her tongue. 'Mind yourself,'

she said. 'Look, Patch, there's a pool and a giant bouncing pillow. Oooh, I can see a bike path through those trees, past the tents. It's over there!'

The bike path. Henry slid down in his seat.

'Sheez, those ponies,' said Patch, pushing them away. One flew up and bounced off the sill and out the car window.

'Hey! Now look what you've done,' said Lulu. 'She's one of my FAVOURITES!' She dropped the other ponies and lunged at Patch's face.

'Yoweeee.' Patch grabbed Lulu by the wrists. 'You need to cut those nails, tiger!'

'I'm not a tiger! Let me go,' said Lulu, wriggling and kicking. 'I'm going to get you! I'm going to pluck out your eyes and give them to crows!'

'Wow. Watch out!' Patch darted forward and seized a handful of ponies and tossed them up. 'Reach for the sky!'

'HEY!' cried Lulu.

A purple pony bounced off Henry's head and into the front of the car. 'Ow!' he groaned, rubbing his forehead.

'Hello, there.'

A girl about Henry's age was peering in through the car window. Her brown hair was a squabble of tangles and her nose was freckled and pink-tipped from too much sun. 'Is this yours?' She held up a yellow pony by the tail.

15

'Not mine!' said Patch, holding up his hands.

'Yes,' said Lulu, reaching out to take the pony. 'That's Marigold! You saved her! THANK YOU!'

The girl rested her elbow on the windowsill. 'Whoah! That's a lot of ponies.'

'Yes,' said Patch. 'Too many.'

'My brother is ANNOYING!'

'Which brother?' said the girl.

Lulu pointed at Patch. 'The big one.'

'Ah,' said the girl. 'What about the other one?'

'They're both naughty,' said Lulu, shaking her head. 'I'm the only good one.'

'Pig's bum,' said Patch, with a snort.

'See?' said Lulu. 'He even says RUDE words!'

The girl laughed. 'That *is* terrible!'

'I'm Lulu. And this is Patch.' Lulu scrunched up her nose at her older brother. She pointed and rolled her eyes. 'And this is Henry.'

Henry tried not to stare at the girl. But her eyes were tawny bright and gold and they reminded him of the sheeny wings of a Christmas beetle.

'Who owns the bike?' asked the girl.

Lulu peered through the window. 'Which bike?'

'The silver one.' The girl turned her head. 'The one on the back of the trailer.'

'Ah – well, that belongs to Henry.' Lulu sniffed the mane of her pony.

'Very cool.' The girl grinned at Henry. 'Maybe we

could go for a ride sometime?'

'Oooooooh, Henry!' said Patch, lifting an eyebrow.

The girl wrinkled her nose. 'You're right, Lulu! Your older brother *is* rude.' She smiled at Patch. A musk pink crept across his cheeks.

'I know,' said Lulu. 'He's preposterous!'

The girl laughed and glanced over at Henry. 'See you round like a rissole,' she said. She pushed off from the car and Henry realised then that she had been balancing on a crimson bike the whole time.

'What sort of bike is that?'

'A dragster,' said the girl.

Lulu shoved her head out the window. 'And how long are you staying?' she cried.

'Probably forever,' called the girl, waving a hand as she swerved around a speed bump and the red and white boom gate.

'Forever?' Lulu asked Henry. 'I thought this place was just for holidays.'

'I don't know,' said Henry, leaning forward between the seats. He watched the girl ride away between the tents, down towards the water and the bike path.

Their dad opened the car door and hopped in. 'Sorry about that. It took forever! They couldn't find the darn booking, for heaven's sake.'

'Thank you for waiting so patiently,' said Mum.

17

'Oi!' Dad sat bolt upright and slid a flattened purple pony out from beneath his bottom. 'Who put this here?'

'Patch!' said Lulu, with a scowl.

'You've got to stop playing with ponies, mate. How many times do I have to tell you?' Their dad chuckled at his own joke and started the car. He drove up to the boom gate and punched in a code. The gate joggled upwards and they drove past a small blackboard advertising a Sunday night Lions barbecue.

The estuary glittered in the distance. Henry wondered about the girl on the crimson dragster. The moment she'd popped her freckled face into the car, it was like the sun had burst through the clouds. Even thinking about her, he found himself wanting to sit up straighter and taller. Was it possible to meet someone for the very first time and feel like you had always known them? Or was that just plain, silly preposterousness?

The RiGHT SORT of COURAGE

'Well, hey, hey, hey!' Mr Barone poked his head out of his trailer and clapped his hands. 'The Hooblers have arrived. Hello, slowcoaches!'

'Why, thank you. Thank you!' said Dad. He leapt out of the car and bowed with a grand flourish.

'The funnies,' said Kale Barone, toddling about in a circle, a fishing net jammed tight on his head.

'Ooh, yes,' said Mrs Barone, coming over to hug Henry's mum. 'So glad you're here! Isn't this place great? I had no idea it was going to be this beautiful.'

'All together at last,' said Dad, shaking hands with Mr Barone and Mr Carson.

Mrs Carson dropped the tennis racquets she was carrying and raced over to Henry's mum. 'You made it!' she cried.

'In one piece,' said Mum. 'But what a drive!
I went through two whole bags of barley sugar.'

They laughed and kissed cheeks. 'Hope you're
feeling ready for our first ever joint family camping
trip?' said Mrs Carson, giving a little grimace of mock
terror.

'Of course.' Mum gave Mrs Carson a reassuring
pat. 'I'm certain it's going to be lovely!' She paused
for a second. 'Although I keep thinking I've left
something crucial behind.'

'Well, as long as you remembered the kids,' said
Mr Carson.

'Tick!' said Dad, with a chuckle. 'Though it was a
close call.'

'Not to mention Lulu's ponies?' added Mrs Carson.

'Ooooh yes,' said Mum. 'We've got the whole
team here—'

'In all of their aromatic glory!' said Dad, tapping
his nose.

Dylan Barone loped over to the car and lunged
through the back window. He wore a singlet top and
was all olive skin and long limbs. His baseball cap was
tilted up. He and Patch slapped hands. 'Dude,' he
said. 'What took you so long?'

Patch glanced at Henry, and then shrugged. 'Bad
traffic.'

'We left early,' said Dylan, grinning. 'Even had
time for a swim along the way.'

20

'And a fish!' hollered Reed Barone, rushing up. 'I nearly caught a snapper.'

'Aaaah, you did not,' said Dylan. 'That was just your overactive imagination.'

'I'm going to catch all sorts of fish this holiday,' said Reed, pretending to hold an invisible bending fishing rod. 'Maybe some albacore, a bream or a tailor. Maybe even some trevally or flounder. But the fish I really want is a kingie out from the island. Oooooh, yeah, bring it on!' He pointed out to sea. 'They're out there in the deep, on the reef, never knowing they're gonna be on the end of my fishing line before the end of the week.'

'Enough about the kingfish already,' said Dylan. 'It's been six hours straight of kingfish and Dad singing Elvis and Mum wondering if she locked the back door. I tell ya, I'm at my limit.'

Lulu leant over to glare at Reed. 'Ha!' she said. 'Catching a big fish is nothing! I'm going to swim in the deep end of the pool and put my head RIGHT UNDER THE WATER.'

'Nah, you won't,' said Reed. 'You'll have to swim in the hot wee wee toddler pool with Kale forever.'

'Will not!' Lulu shook her pink pony in Reed's direction. 'Because Kale is just a baby who still wears nappies!'

'What are you going to do these holidays?' asked Dylan, nodding at Patch.

Patch rubbed his nose. 'I don't know. Might learn to surf. Be good to stand up.'

'They've got a skate park,' said Dylan. 'Reckon I'll give that a whirl.'

'What about you, Hennie?' Reed poked his head through the crook of Dylan's arm. 'What special thing you gonna do that you've never done before?'

'Henry's going to ride his new silver bike,' said Lulu.

'Hah!' said Reed. 'He will not. That's a big boy bike! He's too little for that.'

'Without training wheels!' said Lulu.

'Shhh, Lulu.' The problem with Reed was he had an opinion about everything and once he got started, it was hard to get him to stop.

'Haaah, what? You don't still need training wheels, do you?' Reed slapped his hand against the car door and laughed out loud. 'Are you still some crazy baby or something?'

Henry shook his head. He should have stayed home in his hidey-hole and pinned all his hopes on the kindness of Mrs Neale from next door. He wasn't sure eating bucketloads of gelato and playing a zillion board games was going to be enough to make up for having to put up with smartypants Reed for ten days straight.

'Shut up, eejit,' said Dylan, squeezing Reed's head.

'Yeoww!' said Reed. 'I'll tell Mum!'

Dylan sniffed. 'Whatever.'

'Henry's going to ride a real big boy bike and that's better than catching a big fish! So there, you ninny head!' Lulu kicked the seat in front.

A wave of hotness rolled through Henry. 'Just be quiet!' he said, nudging Lulu fiercely. 'You don't have to tell everybody everything!'

'Hells bells, why are you such a cranky-pants, Lulu Hoobler?' said Reed.

'*Neigh!*' Lulu reared her ponies menacingly at both Reed and Henry.

Dylan opened the car door. 'You want to kick a footy, Patch?' he asked. 'Jay's here but he doesn't want to do anything yet. Just hang round with Carey in the car and read comics.'

'Nah, sorry, guys,' said Dad, jogging towards them. 'No riding or kicking or fishing just yet. It's time to unpack the car and set up the tent. Time to build a home.'

'There's a storm brewing at the back of the inlet,' said Mr Barone, with a groan. He wiped his forehead.

'Ooooh yeah,' said Dad, gazing back. 'Looks a big 'un.' He threw the keys to the trailer up in the air and caught them in the palm of his right hand. 'It's a race then.'

'It's on for young and old,' called Mr Carson, with a grin.

Mum clapped her hands. 'Let's get cracking.'

'Do you want to lend me a hand getting your bike off the rack, Heno?' asked Dad, waving a key in the window.

The roof and doors, pillows and the stench of perfumed ponies pressed in on Henry. A raggedy flutter started up in his chest. 'No thanks,' he said, hunching down.

Patch hopped out of the car. 'I'll give you a hand, old man.'

'Well, that could make an old man break into a song and dance routine,' said Dad, shuffling his feet.

'Don't get overexcited,' said Patch, with a snort.

Henry fiddled with the neckband of his T-shirt. He wished with all his might that his stupid bike had fallen off the back of the trailer. That right now it was resting in some deep thicket of bush where it could never be found.

'Here it is, Heno.' Patch whizzed past the open car door, a silver streak.

The moths whirred in Henry's chest. 'Great,' he murmured, dipping his head between his knees.

Tap, tap, tap. The hammers rang out, pegs biting through the grass. Clouds thickened and swirled over the big blue mountain.

'Come on,' cried Dad. 'Faster. Faster!'

'Keep an eye on Kale,' called Mum. She darted back and forth, stretching and tightening the long lines of rope, trying to peg down the tent, shivering in the breeze. 'Don't let him wander off, Henry. You help too, Lulu.'

'Make sure he looks after Peony, Henry!' commanded Lulu, from the boot of the car. 'I'm only *lending* her to him. It's not for keeps. I want her back.'

'Okay, Lulu,' said Henry. 'I heard you.'

'You're doing a great job, Heno,' said Mrs Barone, dashing past with a basket, her red curly hair springy with sweat. 'Keep it up. That boy's an escape artist. We should have called him Houdini.'

Henry took Kale's sticky hand and led him to the open grass near the bike path.

'I sit you?' asked Kale.

Henry nodded. 'Sure. Okay,' he said.

Kale flopped down onto Henry's lap. His head smelt sweet, like an overripe mango.

'Don't let him lose her, Henry!' called Lulu.

'It's okay, Lulu. You don't have to keep saying the same thing.'

Kale galloped the pink pony over his chubby,

dirty knees. 'You kiss?' he asked, holding the pony up to Henry's lips.

Henry pushed the pony away. 'Ah, not today! No thanks!' He wiped a dollop of spittle from his cheek.

'Don't let him eat it, Henry!'

'I'm not letting him eat it, Lulu!' Henry shrugged. But gosh, what was the point of making a pony smell like a strawberry tart if you didn't want someone to eat it?

Lulu carried another box of ponies out from the car. 'I need to show these ones their new home,' she called, ducking into the tent. 'I'll be back in a minute.'

Henry gazed up and down the bike path. He wondered about the girl on the crimson dragster. Did she *live* in a tent? What would that feel like? Would living here be like always being on holidays or would she hardly even notice anymore?

Kale stood up. 'Me go walk.' He donked the pony against his nose and ambled off along the grass in front of a long line of tents facing out towards the water.

'Hey!' said Henry. 'Wait up.'

Every now and again there was a gap between the tents, like a missing tooth, with a faded yellow grassy patch waiting for a new tent and family to move in. And directly behind was the second line of

26

tents hugging the shade of the pine trees. Everything tucked up close and snug.

'Come back, Kale,' said Henry.

Kale pointed up. 'Bird!' he said, shaking his pony.

'Yep,' said Henry, gazing up at a seagull. He pondered the tall pine trees. Maybe they should be setting their tent further forward? Perhaps it would be better if they all moved to a waterfront tent site, either side of the Carsons? Maybe he should mention this to his dad and to Mr Barone? Then they could talk to the front desk people at Yelonga Inlet Haven. Lightning liked tall pointed objects best, that's what he had learnt. Especially trees because they were full of moisture. Sometimes lightning could zap the sap inside a tree and make it boil so fierce and fast, it blew up the whole tree like a stick of dynamite!

'Bike,' said Kale. He wandered over towards a trike lying abandoned on the grass.

Henry hurried after him.

Didn't his Nonna crawl underneath the dining room table as soon as a storm hit? Everyone knew why she was there, even though she made up the same funny excuse every time, like she was still, after all these years, searching for a missing diamond from her mother's engagement ring, small as a chip of ice.

If there was going to be a storm, Henry hoped there was going to be rain. A lot of rain, first! Enough to soak the trees right through, because if they were completely soggy, it was much less likely they'd be hit by lightning.

'Me have turn,' said Kale, picking up the trike and setting it upright. He swung his little leg over the seat.

'No…no…that's not yours! Don't touch.' Henry rushed over. He grasped Kale's hand.

'He can have a ride,' called a woman wearing a pretty headscarf. 'It's no problem!' She was scrubbing a barbecue out the front of her tent, with a scourer and a bucket. She glanced over her shoulder and shuddered. 'Inshallah, God willing, that big storm goes its own way. Somewhere else. Yes?'

'Yes,' said Henry, suddenly overcome by a rush of shyness.

A bunch of teenage girls swooshed down the bike path, in a cloud of coconut sunscreen. Their thongs snocked loudly against their heels and they were elbowing each other and giggling, their hands cupped over their mouths.

'He's a cutie!' Henry heard one of them murmur.

'How old is your brother?' called a girl with a swinging brown plait.

Henry pretended not to hear. The roof of his mouth felt dry.

'Yeee-heee!' Kale swung on Henry's hand, as if it was a vine and he was a monkey. Henry staggered forwards, nearly falling over.

'Chasey!' Kale called, slipping away.

Henry pretended to run very fast, hurtling after Kale, glad to get away from those confident big girls. Why did they always travel in clumps?

'Can't me catch!' Kale scurried fast on his chubby legs, past neat and sparkly tents, with tidy entrances and everything in its right place.

'I'm going to get you!' said Henry, chasing Kale around a messy tent strewn with buckets, scattered shoes, surfboards and skateboards, like a higgledy-piggledy obstacle course.

'I too fast!' cried Kale.

Henry ducked beneath a makeshift string clothesline, flapping with stripy swimming cozzies and rash shirts and damp towels. Kale squealed and squealed.

'Hey, slow down. Not near the road!' Henry clambered over wobbly pine roots, scaly as old birds' feet. 'Stop! Freeze! STOP!'

A white ute drove up the gravel road, a huge boat strapped onto the trailer behind it. Music doof-doofed so loud it shook the the ground beneath their feet.

'Big boat!' said Kale.

'Yes,' said Henry, breathing out a deep sigh of relief. He grabbed hold of Kale's sweaty, grubby hand. 'Now come away from here.'

There were huge tents with fridges and toasters

and kettles and lamps and even televisions. He
wondered what his mum would make of that! She was
not so fond of screens of any sort, especially on
holidays.

They had come to the end of the long line of
tents but there was still no sign of the girl on the
crimson dragster. Maybe she lived in one of the cabins?

A group of bikies stood by their tents, folding
their gleaming motorbikes in grey tarps, as if
they were wrapping babies in blankets. 'Big storm
coming!' said the biggest bikie, scratching his steel-
wool beard.

A long growl of thunder rumbled from the back
of the inlet.

'Yes,' said Henry, shuddering. He bit his lip.
'Let's go, Kale. Come on.'

Kale itched his nose. 'It rain snails?'

'What?'

'The white ones!' Kale pointed up at the sky.

'Oh,' said Henry. 'You mean *hail.*'

'Yes,' said Kale.

'Hmmm!' said Henry. 'Well?' He turned and
glanced at the clouds roiling towards them. He
scratched his head. Hail!

Of course there couldn't be just the problem
of his bike to worry about, and bugs and spiders
and snakes and stingers and blue-ringed octopi and
tsunamis and sharks and stingrays and whale sharks.

Of course there had to be hail too! What if the hail was as large as giant meteors? Should they go and sit in the car, with the windows up?

A gust of wind blew hard, lifting small twigs and leaves and filling the tents like balloons. A palm tree rustled overhead. Everyone was popping out of their tents now, pulling a line here, re-anchoring a line there, hammers starting up, dinging and ringing, like a bunch of miners digging for gold.

'Kites!' said Kale, pointing.

'Not kites,' said Henry. 'Tents!' He held on to Kale's hot, plump, sticky fingers even tighter. Gosh, what if the wind just snatched Kale straight up and zoomed him away? How could he ever explain that to Mrs Barone?

A bright, alfoil flash of light sparked across the sky.

Holy Zingaroley!

'Let's run,' Henry said.

Kale slumped to the ground. 'No, no, me no go!' he cried. 'Me go bike now! Back! Go back!'

'Later.' Henry tried to scoop Kale up but he was slippery as jelly.

'Bike!' howled Kale, kicking his legs.

Another crack of thunder echoed around the inlet. Dark clouds were sweeping low now. Out past the estuary, in the channel, the water was rimmed with white horses and boats were swivelling wildly on their buoys.

'Me ride!' cried Kale. 'My turn! NOW!' He punched the grass with his fists. Henry gazed about helplessly. Holy Tamoley! Toddlers were more changeable than the weather, going from clear and sunny to cyclone in a matter of minutes.

'Kale.' Henry crouched by his side. 'Please!'

Then came roaring as if a train was bearing down over the mountain, and a rush of wind so fierce even Kale's eyelashes flickered.

'Please, Kale! Come on!'

Cups, newspapers, bowls, sunscreen, hats, dust, sticks and boogie boards cartwheeled around them. People came bolting from every direction; chasing belongings, holding down tarps, splashing out through the reeds, wading into the estuary to collect kids on canoes before they were swept away.

FLASH!

Henry heaved Kale up like a sack and began to run, his heart beating in his chest like a hummingbird. How close was the storm? He needed to count the seconds between the lightning and the rolls of thunder. If the lightning and thunder came close together, he'd know the storm was right above them.

One hippopotamus, two hippopotamus, three hippopotamus, four hippopotamus, five hippopotamus—

But wait a second! Was that right? Maybe it should be hippopotami?

BANG! There came the thunder! Yoweee!

Henry ran faster, Kale's legs flailing about like they belonged to a rag doll. What if they both got struck by lightning? Was that Kale's hair standing up on end? Was a strike imminent? Maybe Henry needed to crouch down now and rest on the balls of his feet? It was hard to tell. Maybe Kale's hair was just sticking up because he was being jiggled around like a bag of potatoes?

FLASH!

One hippopotamus, two hippopotami, three hippopotami, four hippopotami, five hippopotami—

BANG!

Strange facts began to float through Henry's mind. How lightning was six times hotter than the sun! How at any moment there were about fifty flashes of lightning somewhere in the world! How the mountain village of Kifuka in the Democratic Republic of Congo was one of the most-struck places on earth, with an average of one hundred and fifty-eight strikes per year!

FLASH!

One hippopotamus, two hippopotami, three hippopotami—

BANG!

The sky was looking strangely greeny-yellow now and raindrops were landing on Henry's face like small slaps. If it was going to hail, maybe he should think about leaving his bike out in it? Henry had heard hail could damage a car so badly it couldn't even be driven anymore. Maybe the same could happen to a bike? At least that was a comforting thought.

FLASH!

One hippopotamus, two hippopotami—

BANG!

They were almost there. Henry felt Kale sliding through his arms. Who knew one small kid could be so heavy? He could see their three tents though, all set up now and covered by large silver tarps, huddled close like comforting igloos in a snowstorm. He wanted to burst into tears of rejoicing. He hauled Kale higher. And just as he was about to dive in under his tent tarp, he saw her.

The crimson dragster girl was weaving her bike along the bike path, all on her own, like she had all the time in the world. He wanted to shout out a warning, to let her know she should get under cover and stay away from metal, hills, backpacks, open fields, boats, tractors, puddles and corded telephones! But wait a second! The crimson dragster girl wasn't even wearing a bike helmet. Maybe she was a crazy daredevil? Maybe she was one of those loopy storm chasers he had seen on television?

FLASH!

One hippopotami—

BANG!

Henry turned and bolted under the tarp into the tent. He flung Kale to the ground, hurled a sleeping-bag over them both and closed his eyes.

BANG!

BANG!

BANG!

'Don't just stand there looking, sunshine,' shouted Dad, from outside the tent. 'Grab that corner. Quick!'

'I am!' cried Patch, over the howling wind.

'Hold it! Blast and damnation! With both hands! Stop worrying about your hair!'

'Get back inside, Lulu!' yelled Mum. 'I've already told you once. And zip everything up.'

'It's going to flood, Henry!' exclaimed Lulu, from their parent's side of the tent. 'Maybe we're just going to float away like Noah's ark!'

FLASH!

BANG!

FLASH!

BANG!

The wind roared outside. The tarp whipped and flapped like a giant angry bird. The tent strained and groaned, the walls sucking in and out.

'Maybe a tornado is coming!' gasped Lulu.

It could be true! Henry was pretty sure this was no ordinary storm. The dark, greenish-yellow sky. The wind like a freight train. The whirling dust. Oh, gosh, what if all the pegs pinged and the tent took off? Just lifted up and flew away like Dorothy's house in *The Wizard of Oz*?

Henry bunkered down into the moist darkness of his sleeping bag cave, waiting for it all to be over. He'd been so worried about the problem of his bike and bugs and spiders and snakes and stingers and blue-ringed octopi and tsunamis and sharks and whale sharks, when all along what he should have been worried about was hail and lightning and floods and tornadoes!

Kale tapped him on his nose. 'Pony gone,' he whispered.

'What!' A stab of horror winced right through Henry. He dug around, searching desperately behind Kale's sweaty back and beneath his legs.

'It no here!'

'Are you sure?'

'Yes,' said Kale, with a mournful sniff. 'Pony gone, gone.'

Holy Palomino! Kale must have accidentally dropped it. Lulu's pony was out in the storm, facing lightning, wind, hail and floods all on her own. That fresh, sweet-smelling, expecting-the-best-of-everyone strawberry-pink pony.

Oh, gosh, telling Lulu was going to be worse than facing the problem of his silver bike. Worse than facing a teeming bunch of bugs, spiders, snakes, stingers, blue-ringed octopi, tsunamis, sharks, stingrays, whale sharks, hail, lightning, floods and tornadoes all at once!

Henry should go out into the wild storm to rescue that poor pink pony. He should dash out and be brave and noble! He should be a daredevil, like the girl on the crimson dragster! But how could he, when he didn't have an ounce of the right sort of courage?

The VERY WORST THING

'Do you think my pony will be in China by now?' asked Lulu. She swivelled on her stool and gazed out the shop window at the bright orange-and-gold sky.

'No,' said Mum, licking her spoon. 'I don't.'

'Maybe tomorrow she will arrive on the wind and ride in a rickshaw and gallop along the Great Wall?'

'Oh, Lulu,' said Mum.

'She'll probably eat rice noodles and find another little girl to love and I will never see her again.'

'Oh, try to enjoy your gelato, Lulu! It's not often you get to have it for dinner,' said Dad.

'I'm having bubblegum and raspberry sorbet.' Lulu swirled her gelato dolefully around her cup. 'Even though they are not my favourite. Because they are pink. Like Peony.'

'Oh, dog-goggles,' said Patch. 'It's just a dumb pony. It's not like you don't have twenty more of them.'

'It's not just a pony!' Lulu grew bright red. 'You don't know anything.'

Mum nodded. 'Okay. That's enough, Patch.' She stroked Lulu's hair. 'I'm sure Peony will show up in the morning, when everyone has had some time to do a bit of sorting. Try not to worry, Lulu.'

Henry dropped his spoon. It was hard to eat his gelato when he was sitting across from Lulu's glum face.

'But what if she's gone forever?' said Lulu. 'And how will I tell the other ponies?'

'Maybe you could make up a Wanted poster?' Patch bit the end of his waffle cone.

'Or a Lost notice,' said Mum. 'That's probably better.'

Lulu swirled her gelato. 'But I don't have a reward.'

'You could always offer up Henry,' said Patch, wiping his mouth and grinning. 'Seeing the pony got lost on his watch.'

'Oh, Patch.' Mum scooped up a drip of cherry coconut ripple. 'Now you're just being a troublemaker.'

Henry gazed down at the caramel and real banana and broken biscuits and crunchy peanuts.

He wasn't sure he could eat the rest, which was a shame because it had taken him ages to choose. His mum had persuaded him to try a double scoop of plain vanilla and the curiously named banoffee, because she reckoned it was always a wise thing to choose a little taste of home and a little taste of adventure. It was strange how something so light and sweet could suddenly turn so sticky and heavy.

'Mine's delish,' said Patch. 'Chocolate peanut crunch is da bomb, I'm telling you. Yummo.'

'Well, was that four seasons in a day, or what?' asked Dad, shaking his head. He drummed his hands against his stomach and grinned with satisfaction.

Mum squeezed Henry's shoulder. 'Eat up, Heno. Everything will be okay. Peony will turn up, I'm sure of it.'

'I'll eat yours if you can't finish,' said Patch, clicking his fingers under Henry's nose.

Henry slid his gelato cup quickly out of reach. No meal was secure around Patch now. His glittering seagull eyes hovered over every plate, waiting for the moment when he could lunge forward and scoop up last bites and leftovers.

'Look at it this way,' said Dad, gazing outside. 'The worst has happened. And the best is yet to come.'

Henry mushed his spoon through his gelato, turning it into a gloop. How could his dad be so certain? How could he know? What if the storm was just the *beginning* of all their troubles?

Mum dabbed her lips with a serviette. 'The tent stayed up. The tarp stood strong. We are damp but undefeated.'

Lulu double-sniffed. 'Peony probably got sizzled up by the lightning.' Her eyes glimmered with real tears. 'And the only thing left is a single strand of her tail!'

Henry pushed his gelato cup across the table. 'You can have it,' he said, shaking his head.

'Yipp-ee,' said Patch, his voice suddenly splintering into a loud squawk. He scooped a giant dollop straight into his mouth. 'Oh, banoffee is superb. I can't believe you can't finish it. What's wrong with you? Hmmm...mmmm. This is a mouthful of paradise.'

After Henry had been to the bathroom to clean his teeth, he slid into his sleeping-bag. He popped his lantern down just behind his pillow.

Lulu was already sound asleep, breathing through her mouth, tiny beads of sweat on her forehead. A long line of Little Ponies kept watch along the edge of the tent. The whites of their eyes glinted, even in the shadows.

Patch lay on his side, tapping away on his phone. Outside, there was the clatter of dice on a

41

table, the clink of bottles and the gentle babble of voices. His mum was moving here and there in the camp kitchen, her shadow stretching and shrinking against the skin of the tent. 'Lights off, Heno,' she murmured.

Henry switched his lantern off.

A soft breeze swelled through the tent. It was like living in an animal. It was like being flat bang in the middle of a giant lung or something.

Lulu snored and turned over, planting her hand smack against his cheek. Henry lifted it off and tucked it beneath her sleeping-bag.

The corellas meowed mournfully in the pine trees. How could his dad be so confident that the best was yet to come? Did he just pretend that there were no bugs and spiders and snakes and stingers and blue-ringed octopi and sharks and stingrays and whale sharks out there? Or did he just forget? Because there it was now – the ocean – roaring in the distance. How come it was so loud, when Henry hadn't noticed it all afternoon? What if a tsunami came rolling in? Would the breakwaters be enough to hold it back? Where would he run to first? Should he climb a tree? Or the roof of a building? Climb the tennis nets? Or make for the hill?

Who would look after Lulu? She wouldn't leave unless she gathered up all the ponies first. And boy, imagine if another one got lost! She'd make the hugest fuss, chuck the world's biggest tantrum and she wouldn't leave without it and the next thing you know the water would be tumbling them about like they were a bunch of odd socks in a washing machine. Maybe he should pack those ponies into their boxes right now, just in case?

Henry sighed. When his thoughts began to blizzard, his dad would scruff his hair and say, 'Now, now, Mr Worst Case Scenario! Let's settle it down.' He took another deep breath.

'You gonna try that bike of yours tomorrow?' asked Patch, rolling over.

A cloud of moths rose up in Henry's chest. 'Not sure,' he murmured.

'It's a cool bike,' said Patch, sliding his phone underneath his Therm-a-Rest.

Henry lay on his back, paralysed with dread.

The bike. It was not cool. It was the very worst thing. It was his biggest problem, even more terrifying than bugs and spiders and snakes and stingers and blue-ringed octopi and tsunamis and sharks and stingrays and whale sharks!

That bike would be waiting for him the next day and the day after that and the day after that one. It would be with him forever. Nothing could shake it off. Everyone would always be asking him about it, waiting for the moment when he was meant to conquer it.

43

'I could teach you.'

Henry snatched up the hood of his sleeping bag and squeezed it tight around his head. He didn't want to think about the bike. He didn't want to think about it at all. 'I'll see.'

'Whatever,' grunted Patch, rolling away.

But then a new thought struck Henry. What if someone wandered through the holiday park and *stole* his bike? What if they snipped the chain and rode off on it?

Good gravy...that would be one Worst Case Scenario he would love! It would be some kind of miracle! He crossed his fingers and wished with all his might for a crafty thief to come.

The tarps whispered on the breeze.

Henry heard them rise and fall, rise and fall, rise and fall, until his thoughts slowed right down and he was lulled, at last, into a deep sleep.

A KNIGHT
on a
SHINING BIKE

The screeching of lorikeets woke Henry early. His mouth was dry as a desert and he was desperate to go to the bathroom. He slid out of his sleeping bag and tiptoed around Lulu and her ponies, which seemed to have scattered all over the floor in the night, like wild brumbies on the run. He unzipped the tent and fly and crawled through the small hole. His dad was sitting on a camp chair near the edge of their tarp, holding a mug of coffee in his hand. He was staring out at the water, toasting his hairy legs in the sun.

'Hello, early bird,' he whispered. 'You sleep well?'

'Sure,' said Henry.

'I've staked out the joint,' said Dad. 'I've been for a long bike ride already and there's a stack to see. Stingrays, seals, Nugget Rock shining like fool's gold

45

and on the other side, the inlet so glassy and smooth, a fishing paradise...'

Reed slid out from the tent opposite in his pyjamas, bed-haired and bleary-eyed like he had just slithered from a cocoon. 'Sunny!' he whispered, looking up. 'Yay!' He tugged at his pyjama pants, pulling them up high. 'Who wants a bowl of Coco Pops?'

The smell of burnt toast and bacon drifted in the air.

'Nah,' said Henry, jiggling on the spot. 'No thanks.'

'How about we tackle your bike?' said Dad. 'Get a quick lesson in before breakfast?'

Henry swallowed. No crafty thief had come in the night. There it was: the bike. He couldn't escape it. He glanced at Reed.

'Yeah!' said Reed, licking his lips. 'Whatcha waiting for, Hennie?'

Henry shook his head. 'Not now,' he mumbled.

'I'd sure love to ride around with you to Nugget Rock,' said Dad. 'I saw a baby seal round there this morning, slapping a fish.'

'Maybe later,' said Henry. 'I need to go to the bathroom now.'

'I'll go with you, Mr Hoobler,' said Reed, with a smirk. 'After I've gone for a fish first.'

'Ah, well, maybe later then,' said Dad, with a tiny sigh.

Henry slunk away quickly, the grass wet beneath

his feet. Gosh, that Reed! What was wrong with him? He was into everything. Maybe he'd grow up to be like Mr Duffy from across the road, wandering the streets on council pick-up day, fossicking through the trash on everyone's front lawn, searching for hidden treasure.

Because, after all, Henry wanted to do stuff with his dad. He did. But his dad was so...what did his mum always say? Exuberant. Yes, that was the word. His dad was exuberant, which meant enthusiastic and some other word, what was it again...buoyant. Yes, buoyant as a boat, as if nothing would ever sink him. Mostly, this was a good thing. Like when Henry first went to school and was scared he might never learn to read, his dad's confidence gave Henry courage, even when the words in the readers jumped and blurred together.

But the bad thing about his dad's exuberance for everything was that he was so loud. He was into celebrating and rejoicing, whoo-hooing and clapping every new little step, every tiny gain.

Learning to ride a bike was different from learning how to read.

Henry wanted to learn quietly, without any fuss, far away from all his friends and family, where no one he knew could see his mistakes or his fear.

Henry took the long way back from the bathroom. He cut between the ritzy-ditzy cabins, the ones his dad reckoned cost twelve arms and twelve legs to stay in. He trod carefully around the scaly roots of the pine trees and stepped out onto the footpath.

Early morning joggers rushed by, their feet pounding. Scruffy dogs tugged at their leads, sniffing the salty air. Bellbirds ting-tinged from across the water.

Everyone was happy and polite and said things like 'Morning!' and 'Lovely day' and smiled at him, as if it was not unusual to see a boy in his pyjamas taking a stroll on a public footpath.

Henry paused to gaze over the water. A flock of birds rose up suddenly from out near a tiny island. They flew so tightly and close it was like watching one big bird, rather than hundreds of small ones. They dipped and turned, rising up and then sweeping left, the flash of their wings creamy white. Then they skimmed the water and whizzed up again, as if they didn't know how to settle.

Just then Henry heard a splash. A different bird popped its head out of the water and then flew up and struck down again. A school of fish sprang out in silvery arches – once, twice, three times – down towards the bridge.

Henry lunged forward, straining to see more. Ah, that poor bird! He was like a cartoon character, diving in and coming up empty every single time, those tiny fish sticking close together, quicker than a bunch of quavers.

'Wow,' he breathed, turning to see if anyone else had noticed.

The girl on the crimson dragster bike was perched right behind him. 'Ha!' she said, with a grin. 'My Nan reckoned the best things always happen on the way to somewhere else.'

'Is that right?' said Henry.

'Yep. For sure!' said the crimson dragster girl. 'Take last night – I was going for a ride after the storm when I saw something out of the corner of my eye. So I stopped to take a look and found this.' She reached into her bike basket and pulled out a strawberry-pink pony.

Henry's stomach flipped like a pancake. 'That's Peony.'

'I thought it might be a member of your family.' The crimson dragster girl lifted her eyebrows high. A small smile fizzed on her lips. 'So tell your little sister I'm her knight on a shining bike!' She tossed the pony to him and flicked her fingers up in a funny greeting that was both hello and goodbye all at once. Then she surged off down the grass and up the path, coasting from side to side, her crimson dragster moving like a dancer, curving left, then right.

Henry stood up straighter. He clutched the pony

tight to his chest and watched her ride away, even though he wanted to tell her to stop. Where had she found Peony? How could he thank her? He wanted to ask her what made her so sure that best things always happen on the way to somewhere else – how could that be true?

But then he remembered that the girl had seen his *pyjamas*, the exploding rockets, shooting stars and planets, so now she would be thinking he was nothing but a baby. Good grief, why didn't he get changed before going to the bathroom, or at the very least wear pyjamas without a pattern? Now he couldn't get back to the tent quick enough.

'Hey there.' Reed ambled towards Henry. He wore bright blue board shorts and a surfie singlet. A fishing rod rested against his shoulder and he was swinging a red bucket. 'So,' he cried, scrunching up his nose. 'Who's the girl, Hennie? Is she your new girlfriend?'

'Just zip it,' said Henry.

'You gonna kiss her, Hen?' Reed clucked like a chicken.

Henry brushed past, shaking his head. He didn't have any words handy that could express the fullness of his scorn.

Why couldn't a boy and a girl just be friends? Why did everyone have to go like a stupid ninny-head the minute a boy and a girl talked for one tiny second? All that dreaming about fish, all that hoping about fish and all that babbling about fish had left Reed with fish flakes for brains.

'Do you see the way she rides that bike?' called Reed. 'She's no scaredy-cat.'

Scaredy-cat. That word sunk inside Henry like a stone. 'What do you know?' he muttered, stomping off up the path.

'Ah, Henny,' chirped Reed. 'I know everything!'

TREASURE

'**B**ut where did she find Peony?' asked Lulu, hugging her pony close.

'I don't know,' said Henry. 'She didn't say.'

Lulu kissed her pink pony's nose. 'It's a miracle.'

'She said to tell you she is your knight on a shining bike.'

'When you see her again, Lulu,' said Mum, looking up from her magazine, 'make sure you say thank you.'

'If I had a zillion billion gold dollars,' said Lulu, 'I would give them all to her!'

Henry gazed out at the bike path, looking for the girl on her crimson dragster, but all he could see were the nuggety rugrats from next door with their spiky helmets, whizzing up and down on their bikes, brazen and loud, shouting out to each other, 'Look at me, no hands! NO HANDS! Whoop! Whoop!'

'Henry,' said Lulu. 'Do you want to come to the pool with me and my ponies?'

'Well,' said Henry, swallowing.

'Pretty please? Pretty please with cream and a cherry on top?'

'Maybe.' Henry kicked off his thongs and slipped into the tent. He had to get out of his pyjamas quick, just in case. He scrabbled through his crate, looking for his board shorts and rash shirt. He got dressed in a corner and then shoved his rocket pyjamas right to the bottom of his crate, beneath his jeans and long-sleeved shirts. When he came out of the tent, he snatched up a banana from the fruit bowl and peeled it fast. 'I'm starving,' he said.

'There are some croissants in the bag on the table, if you want one,' said Mum, sipping her coffee. 'Fresh from the bakery.'

Henry fished out a buttery, flaky croissant. He sat down with his banana and took turns biting from both.

'Your dad's taken Patch for a quick surf at Joe's Beach,' said Mum, glancing up from her crossword. 'Dylan's headed over to the skate park and Reed's going to try his hand fishing on the estuary. I think Jay and Carey might be building Bionicles with Kale in their tent, if that takes your fancy?'

'Not really,' said Henry.

'Well, Lulu and I are going to the pool in a second, so feel welcome to join us.'

Henry nodded. 'Okay.'

'Can we go now? Can we go now?' chanted Lulu, running around in circles, galloping ponies in front.

'Get your hat,' said Mum.

'Yeee–heeee,' said Lulu. She put her ponies down on top of the camp fridge and began rummaging in a bucket. Hats flew everywhere, between her legs, over her shoulders, bouncing off the tent. 'Got it!' she cried, waving a sun hat covered with cherry blossoms.

Mum eased herself up from the table with a big sigh. 'Oh, Lulu,' she said. 'You're incorrigible!'

'Is that good?' asked Lulu.

'That depends.' Mum scooped up her magazine, beach bag and towels. 'Now pack those other hats away.'

Lulu raced about snatching up hats and shoving them back into the bucket. 'Ready!' she cried.

'Okay then,' said Mum.

'Let's go,' said Lulu with a grin, dragging Mum by the hand.

The three of them meandered up past the giant chess set and down the path towards the swimming pool. A big boy opened the gate and Henry darted past a clump of shivering coconut girls on their way out. 'It's freezing today,' said one girl, her lips blue.

Lulu lined up her ponies on the edge of the big pool and jumped straight into the shallow end, while their mum sat nearby on a tan plastic lounge chair, her bare legs covered with a towel.

Henry flopped on the lawn. He plucked at blades of grass, watching ants tumble clumsily up and down, through a scratchy tangle of roots.

'Watch me, watch me,' Lulu shouted.

'I *am* watching,' said Mum.

Lulu dove just beneath the surface, her bottom wiggling like an unsinkable floatie. 'Did you see?' she asked, standing up, swiping her hair back. Her eyes were big behind their goggles. 'Did you see? I put my whole head under!'

'I saw!' said Mum. 'Well done, you clever girl.'

'Heno,' cried Lulu. 'Come in and play with me. Please! Please! Please!'

Henry hesitated. There were no other big brothers playing with their little sisters in the pool.

'Please, Heno. Please!' Lulu clung to the side of the pool. She pushed out her bottom lip.

'Stop staring at me like that,' said Henry.

'Please, Heno,' she said, dipping her head and gazing up at him soulfully. 'I promise to be good and to do exactly what you tell me.'

Henry bit his lip. He was good at playing pretend, and sometimes the stories he made up with Lulu were so real it almost felt as if they were happening. And the longer he played, the less likely it might be that he would have to learn how to ride his bike.

'Okay.' He glanced over his shoulder at the jumping pillow to check for bossy-boots Reed. 'But only if you *listen.*'

'Seahorse, seahorse,' Lulu said. 'Let's play that!'

And so Henry spent the next hour at Lulu's beck and call. He darted about the pool, pretending to be a magical sea pony, with Lulu perched on his back.

They fought the evil sea hag Mibena, who had cast a terrible spell across the whole of the underwater kingdom. They wrestled with her minions, the kraken and sea serpents and sea dragons. They rescued languishing mermaids from their cave prisons and freed selkies, seals, dugongs and turtles from dark underwater dungeons.

Then Lulu vanquished the evil sea hag above a coral meadow, with a simple spell, and peace came to the underwater kingdom again. Only then did Lulu get out of the pool. She sat shivering beside Mum, tired out, wrapped up tight in a My Little Pony towel, waiting to be warmed by the sun.

Palm trees rustled.

The pool was a dark sapphire blue. Henry took a deep breath and sank into the water like a crocodile, so only his eyes popped out.

There were lots of people swimming now. Babies drifted by in yellow ducky rings. In the middle of the pool, two short stubby men with tattooed stars on their backs were throwing children backwards and forwards like basketballs. At the deep end, an older grey-haired lady sat on a ledge, next to a younger lady in a tomato red T-shirt. 'Isn't this lovely, Moira?' cried the grey-haired lady to the red T-shirt lady. 'Aren't we lucky!'

Moira nodded and sat closer to the grey-haired lady, closer than a shadow. Henry could tell Moira had Down Syndrome like Ellie in Year Six at his school.

Henry guessed the grey-haired lady was Moira's mum. But there were two little girls with them too and they were throwing themselves against the grey-haired lady and wrapping their arms around her neck, taking turns to kiss her pale papery cheeks.

Henry wondered if these girls were the grey-haired lady's grandchildren. She looked like a granny to Henry. She had the same sweetness of face, the same creamy, calm expression he recognised in his own Nonna.

'Careful now!' called the grey-haired lady to the little girls. 'You'll knock Aunty Moira off the step.'

Moira sat gazing up at the sky, like she hardly noticed those girls throwing themselves like salmon upstream.

Then the granny dove off the ledge, as if she had suddenly had enough. She swam out into the deep and the two little girls flung themselves after her. 'Granny Apples!' they called, snatching at her arms. 'Apples! Wait! Wait!' And they thrashed down the pool, wide as a three-headed monster. And just like that, Moira popped off the step too and swam after them, one small hand perched up on her head like a fin.

A fin! Henry laughed. He couldn't help it.

Moira was swimming in the deep, with her head right under water. She was swimming down the pool as if she wasn't afraid of anything. She was chasing after her mum and hunting down her two splashy nieces like some sneaky shark and nobody noticed but him! Henry held that funny moment like a small quiet treasure. Everything was shiny because of it, the whole wide world glittering with possibility, waiting to be discovered wherever he might look.

GENIUS

The next morning, rain came early. It stippled down gently at first. Then harder and harder, until it was drumming away, beating against the tarp.

'I'm still going swimming,' Lulu murmured right into Henry's ear at breakfast, her morning breath apple-juice sweet. She was wearing her pyjamas and her goggles, the lenses all foggy.

'Shhh,' said Henry. 'Go away.'

'I don't care if it's freezing,' muttered Lulu. 'I don't have much time. I've got to swim in the deep, in the DEEP, with my head under water. Before the holiday is over. Or Reed will call me *scaredy-cat!*'

Henry flicked a toast crumb off the table. He stared at Reed, who was wolfing down a bowl of cereal at the end of the table. How did he get so good at making everyone so darn scared of being scared?

'Oh dear,' cried Mrs Barone, hugging the sleeves of her jumper tight. She peered out from beneath the tarp, at the grey, grey sky and the falling rain. 'Isn't this miserable? What are we going to *do*?'

'No bike-riding lessons today, champ,' said Dad, grazing his fist gently against Henry's cheek.

Reed slurped his milk straight from the bowl. 'Hope you're not going to run out of days, Hennie.'

Sometimes Henry wished he had a wand or a paintbrush that could turn all annoying people invisible. He glared at Reed and then turned away and gazed out at the weather.

Something light and happy still popped up inside him, though. No bike riding today. One more day of freedom! Who knew that even in the midst of pouring rain there could be such a cheery ray of sunshine?

'Well, I'm off to the laundry to dry the bath and beach towels,' said Mum, 'because every single one is damp or wet through.'

'I'm still going swimming,' said Lulu.

'Are you, tadpole?' said Dad. 'It's a bit wet for that, I'm thinking.'

'I've got to go fishing at some point,' said Reed. 'I need to catch a big kingie. They're out there, I know it, but they're hiding.'

Jay leant on the camp table. 'It's a great day for

reading in the tent. I have a stack of *Asterix* books here, if someone wants to read them. There's a lot of good thumpings in them, and magic, and war—'

'And don't forget *The Calvin and Hobbes Tenth Anniversary Book*,' said Carey.

Patch sat bolt upright. 'I know! Let's eat pancakes! Big golden pancakes. And then...let's play games!'

'Games!' breathed Dylan. 'Yes!'

'A marathon of games!' said Patch. 'Against the...MEN!'

'Pancakes,' cried Jay. 'With maple syrup.'

'And cream!' breathed Lulu.

'Don't forget Nutella!' Carey pretended to karate chop the air.

'Epic games!' said Dylan. 'Of a colossal nature! YES! Bring it on!'

'I'm not playing,' said Carey. 'I've got to finish Calvin.'

Kale danced about in his nappy and gumboots near the edge of the tarp. 'Hot chocolate,' he shouted. 'Hot! Hot! Hot! Now! Now! Now!'

'Come here, nudie rudie,' said Mr Barone, lunging out to scoop Kale up, just as a giant torrent of water ran off the tarp – *sloosh* – directly down the back of his neck. 'Yeeeooooow,' gasped Mr Barone. He stood up straight, his T-shirt wet through. 'Now, that's seriously *cold*!'

'You're soaked, Dad,' said Dylan. 'Sodden!'

'Wash hair, Daddy,' said Kale, sliding his hands through his dad's dripping hair. 'Close eyes!'

The older boys fell about laughing.

'Laugh all you like now, boys,' said Mr Barone. 'But we all know who will laugh last. Bring on the games! And the pancakes! Hot as they come and many of them! On the double. And a thermal blanket too! Silver foil, if possible.'

'You don't ask for much,' said Mrs Barone, folding her arms.

Mr Barone shivered. 'I'm almost hypothermic.'

'Your wish is my command!' said Mr Carson. He plonked an electric frypan down on the table, plugged it in to an extension cord and switched it on. 'Get ready for the world's best pancakes, my friend,' he said to Mr Barone. He shook a pancake bottle up and down, up and down like a giant maraca. Then he poured a perfect pancake, pale as a full moon.

'I think we should start with cards first,' said Patch. 'Maybe a game of Cheat to get warmed up.'

'Warmed up,' said Mr Barone. 'I like it.'

Dylan rubbed his hands together. 'Oooh, yeah, I love Cheat.'

'But don't forget Up the River, Down the River,' said Jay. 'I'm a master at that.'

'And Poohead,' added Reed.

'Yesss!' breathed Patch.

'Can I play too?' asked Henry.

Everyone stopped talking. An awkward silence bloomed. The big boys gazed at their hands and then out towards the distant misty breakwater.

'Nah,' said Reed. He gazed over at Henry with a smug smile and beat his pointy fingers like drumsticks against the table. 'You're too little!'

'Ah, Heno!' said Dad, hesitating. 'Look...I don't know. These games...they've got pretty complicated rules. They're a lot harder than Snakes and Ladders and Steady Eddy and Sleeping Queens and Uno.'

'But I'm good at games,' said Henry. 'I'm telling you, I know how to play.'

'No munchkins allowed!' said Patch. 'They just slow everything down.'

'I'm not a munchkin,' said Henry.

Patch laughed. 'Oooooh, yes, you are!'

'Why don't you and I play a game of Uno when I get back from the laundry?' said Mum to Henry. 'I won't be long! Maybe Lulu and Kale can play with us? And we can let Patch, Jay, Dylan and Reed play the men?'

'But I want to play with the big boys,' said Henry.

'But you can't, because the big boys don't want to play with you!' Patch flicked Henry on the ear.

'Hey, cut that out, Patch!' said Dad. 'Hands off! How many times do I have to tell you?'

'You've got to be double figures to play,' said Reed with a snigger.

'I'm almost double figures,' said Henry.

'Oh, you are not!' said Reed, rolling his eyes.

Lulu poked out her tongue. 'You big old bossy-boots.' She glared at Reed.

'Oh dear,' said Mrs Barone. She plopped two lemons down by the frypan and peeped over Mr Carson's shoulder as he flipped the first pancake. 'Well, you know, I think you should give Heno a chance. We're on holidays! We have nearly all the time in the world, don't we?' She stared at the big boys pointedly. They grunted and peered down at the grass.

'Surely it's now or never to try something a little bit new?' Mrs Barone asked. 'Because I'm pretty sure there were plenty of times when you were given some sort of go. Hmmmm?'

The big boys shifted in their seats. There was a long silence. The pancake gently bubbled on the pan.

'Orright, then.' Dylan tossed a tennis ball and caught it on the full.

'One chance, though,' said Patch. 'That's all he gets.'

Reed sniffed. 'That sounds fair!'

'Oh, Patch! Oh, Reed,' said Mrs Barone. 'I think we can be a little more generous than that, can't we?'

She raised a thin, perfect eyebrow and waited for a long moment.

'Two chances then.' Patch snatched up a deck of cards.

'Voila!' said Mr Carson. 'Here it is! Hot as it comes.'

'Alright, then,' said Mrs Barone. She slid a plastic plate towards Mr Carson. 'I think this first big golden pancake belongs to Henry. And may the best man win!'

The rain drizzled down. It billowed out in clouds of mist. Everything smelt of wet grass and sea.

Dylan shuffled a deck of cards. 'Let's go easy on Heno at first,' he said. 'Okay.'

'No special treatment!' Patch swooshed his fringe to the side, patting it down firmly, like it was an unruly pet.

Reed nodded. 'Yeah! That's right.'

'Don't be such a meanie,' said Lulu, glancing up from her My Little Pony colouring book at the end of the table. A smear of maple syrup shone on her cheek.

Mr Barone strung up a side tarp to shelter them from the incoming rain, while Mr Carson switched on the fairy lights beneath the tarp, even though it was day. Lanterns dotted the table, throwing out rays of buttery light.

Dad slid a bowl of pretzels onto the table. 'Deal

the cards out, Dylan!' he said, grabbing a chair. 'Let's get this show on the road!'

The first game they played was Cheat; it was a race to see who could get rid of all of their cards first. Henry held his cards carefully to his chest and watched everyone closely.

He noticed the way Jay spoke very fast when he was trying to cheat and the way Dad started snatching greedily at the pretzels. Patch tried to look guilty on every turn, stroking his fringe and shifting his eyes like he was a burglar, but when he was really trying to get away with something he bit the inside corner of his mouth. When Mr Barone tried to get rid of his extra cards he jiggled his leg extra quick, and Reed started breathing in little huffs.

Then Henry placed his last cards on the pile and said, 'Two Jacks!'

'Cheat!' shouted Mr Barone. He stretched over and lifted the cards up. Two Jacks stared disdainfully back. Everyone groaned and slumped in their chairs.

'What the heck?' said Reed.

'Oh, wowee,' said Mr Carson. 'We've just been smashed by the puppy!'

Dad tossed his cards on the table. 'The sneaky assassin!' he said, shooting Henry a quick grin.

'Gosh,' said Mr Barone, 'talk about coming from behind.'

Jay ran his hands through his hair. 'But I was so close!'

'Fluke!' said Patch, scooping up the cards and starting to shuffle them.

'Flukey-lukey!' said Reed.

Henry glared. Patch was always tearing the wrapping paper off any big, good thing he said or did. And Reed was like a loud, bad echo.

'How about we can the trash talk,' said Dad, staring at Patch, 'and try another game.'

When Henry won two rounds straight of Up the River, Down the River, followed by two fast rounds of Poohead, there were great moans of disbelief. 'Crikey,' said Mr Barone, sagging in his chair. 'I'll be a monkey's uncle! Where did you get this kid?'

'Blimey!' said Mr Carson, banging his forehead against the table. 'We have just been mauled.'

'Whiz-kid!' Dylan pretended to bow down before Henry. 'Card shark!'

'How did he get so good?' asked Mr Carson. 'Who's been teaching him?'

Henry tapped his fingers on the messy pile of cards. 'Nonna,' he said. 'I play a lot of games with her on Thursday afternoons, when Patch goes to soccer and Lulu goes to dancing.'

'You need to speak to that mother-in-law of yours,' said Mr Barone to Dad. He thumped the table. 'The very least she could do is give *you* some lessons!'

'Nothing's going to save me! Not a million lessons,' said Dad, with a large grin.

'You know, I think Heno's got the magic touch,' said Mum from the end of the table, where she was folding beach and bath towels.

'Abracadabra!' Lulu pointed a texta at Henry.

Mr Barone sighed. 'He's King Midas.'

'Uh-huh,' said Mr Carson, passing along some guacamole dip and a bowl of corn chips. 'Everything he touches turns to gold.'

'Yay, Heno,' cried Mrs Barone, sweeping Kale up onto her hip. 'I'm telling you, he's a *genius*! He's a genius for noticing things!'

Genius!

He knew what that word meant.

It meant brilliant. Or like a mastermind. It was the word his teacher Miss Coale used to describe Andrew Chichester, who could do Year Six maths, even in Year Two. It wasn't a word anyone had ever used to describe Henry, though, and it wasn't a word he'd ever heard anyone use about something as plain and ordinary as *noticing things*! Henry's face was suddenly hot.

'No way! You can't be a genius just because you're good at games,' said Reed, throwing down his cards. 'Just because you're good at noticing something.'

'Well, that's where you're wrong, Reedie,' said

Mr Barone. 'Just look at all the chess champions in the world.'

'Let's give Sequence a go.' Patch grabbed the board game from the crate.

'Bags being on the Genius's team,' said Dylan, scooping guacamole with a corn chip.

'I'm not playing,' said Reed, flushing red. He glared at his brother.

'Come on, mate,' said Mr Carson. 'I'll be on your team.'

Patch snapped the board open and divvied the cards and counters up between the teams. 'Best of three games,' he said, glancing around the group.

Henry and Dylan won the first round. It was like the patterns leapt right up before Henry's eyes, all the straights and diagonals, before anyone else even had a chance to see them. He loved the crisp fresh smell of the cards and the feel of the counters, the ridged edges against his fingers and the bright explosion of colour on the board.

They lost the second game to Patch and Mr Barone. 'Ay, caramba!' shouted Mr Barone, snapping down his green chip. 'At last. Victory!'

Everyone hunched around the board on the third game. They played quietly and quickly at first. Mr Barone laughed maniacally every now and again whenever he or Patch thwarted Henry and Dylan.

Everyone's tummies rumbled and gurgled, but no one paid them any attention. Henry wanted to pray for the magic card, he really did. The excitement in his stomach was as big as Christmas.

'No sniffing,' said Patch to Dylan. 'That's table talk.'

'Oh bull, settle down,' said Dylan. 'I've got a runny nose, you big goober.'

And then it was Henry's turn again and he scooped up the ace of spades. He swallowed and licked his bottom lip.

The winning card was now in his hand, but he needed to keep his face calm. He had to keep a tight lid on all the fizzing. He sighed and glanced away, as if his new card was nothing special, even a little bit disappointing. He gazed at the drips hanging off the edge of the tarp, like tiny icicles.

But Holy Slamoley, why was everyone else suddenly taking so long? Everyone was checking their cards, checking the board, tipping their necks from side to side, checking their cards, checking the board, fingers dithering, as if there was all eternity to play the game. Henry flattened his cards against his chest, as if that might help to keep him from suddenly screaming his head off like a nutso.

'It's your turn now,' said Dad, nodding at Patch.

'I know,' said Patch, glaring back.

'I'm just saying!' said Dad.

70

Patch raised an eyebrow. 'Okay. Whatever.'

'A quick game's a good game.' Dad grinned and tapped his foot against the table leg.

Patch sniffed. 'Enough, Dad!'

'No sniffing,' said Dylan to Patch, with a smirk. 'It's against the rules!'

'Ooooh, it's tense. It's tense here in the stadium tonight, folks!' said Mr Carson, rubbing his hands greedily together. 'It's a colossal match of epic proportions.'

Patch placed a three of hearts and a chip on the board, then picked up a card from the deck.

Henry glanced out the front. He saw the girl on the crimson dragster weaving her way down the bike path through the puddles, water spraying behind her. He wondered where she was going so fast and what best things she might see along the way. But then it was his turn and he laid his card gently down, followed by his chip. 'Voila!' he said, looking around the table.

'What!' Reed stood up.

'Woot!' cried Dylan, leaping up. 'Woot! Woot! There it is. That's magic! It's all over, red rover. We are the champions. High five, buddy!'

Henry slapped his palm against Dylan's outstretched hand.

'Oh, rats,' said Patch, shaking his head. 'Rats, rats, RATS!'

'Well played,' said Mr Barone, ruffling Henry's hair. 'You won that fair and square.'

'All hail the grandmaster!' cried Dylan.

Reed flung his chips down. They bounced off the table and landed in the grass. 'I'm going fishing,' he cried, stomping off.

Mrs Barone marched over to the edge of the tarp. 'You come back here, Reed Barone. RIGHT NOW! Everyone needs to help pack up!'

'NO!'

'Oh, gosh.' Mrs Barone turned back and gazed at the group helplessly.

Lulu looked up from combing her ponies. 'He's incorrigible!'

'Oh, now, Lulu,' said Mum quickly. 'You don't need to say a single thing.'

'But he's being very obtreperosis.'

'That's enough!' said Dad.

They listened to the sound of rain speckling the tarp.

'I'll go,' said Mr Barone, standing up with a sigh. He reached over and shook Henry's hand firmly. 'Thanks for the games, Heno.'

Dad slapped Henry on the back. 'Well done, mate,' he said. 'Well played.'

Mr Carson nodded. 'Great game.'

Patch stood up and stretched his arms over head. 'Okay, Heno,' he said, as he cricked his knuckles.

'Well done, you blooming grand *genius*! Next time, you have to play on my team, alright?'

Henry shrugged. 'Okay.'

'Awesome!' Patch tackled him. 'Because we munchkins need to stick together.' And he gave Henry's head a big tight squeeze.

SURPRISES

That night, Dylan shouted Henry a special three-scoop gelato sundae. 'Here ya go, grandmaster,' he said, sliding it across the table to Henry. 'This is for you. Banoffee, vanilla and cherry coconut ripple. Enjoy!'

'Reed had to stay in the tent,' confided Lulu, 'because he wouldn't say sorry, not even when his mum and dad told him to a hundred times and now he has to miss out and tonight they have pavlova flavour.' She nodded her head vigorously. 'And when he finds out about that I'm pretty sure he will be sorry about not being sorry!'

'Oh, Lulu,' breathed Mum. 'Please!'

Lulu nibbled her waffle cone. 'Maybe some people are just big scaredy-cats about saying an incy-wincy word like *sorry*!' A drip of watermelon gelato hung off her chin.

'Just eat up,' said Mum, reaching over to swipe it away.

'Ow!' wailed Lulu. 'You're *hurting* me!'

Henry scratched his nose. He didn't think sorry was an incy-wincy word. It always felt like a word that weighed a lot. Sometimes after he had done the wrong thing and spoken it out loud, the space still ached where it used to be, in a way that was both happy and sad. He gazed down at his gelato.

'Whoo-heee,' said Dad. 'There's a lot there, Heno. I'll be happy to give you a hand if that gets too much for you.'

'I'll be okay,' said Henry, elbowing his dad away. He ate slowly, savouring every mouthful. Gosh, there were no better flavours! The cherry coconut ripple even had real toasted coconut and dark chocolate chunks.

'It's been a good day, yeah?' said Mum. She licked the drips running down her lemon sorbet waffle cone.

'Yep,' said Henry. 'The best.'

'I hope it doesn't rain tomorrow, but,' said Patch. 'Because I want to get out and surf again. Today was okay, but give me a day with some sun, please.'

Lulu dipped her tongue into her cone. 'But if it rains tomorrow,' she said, her teeth bright pink, 'we can all play the My Little Pony Memory Game.

It's very hard. You have to match the ponies and to do that you have to remember where they are and flip them over and I am very good at making matches.'

'Oh, no!' cried Patch. 'Spare me the giddy-up, partner. I'm trying to forget ponies, not remember them.'

'You big meanie.' Lulu kicked Patch's shin fiercely.

'Owww! She just broke my leg. Did you see that?'

'Settle down, tulips,' said Dad.

'Settle down?' said Patch. 'Do you call that discipline? I'm going to start wearing my hair in pigtails with cute little boggly boos and hug a pony, if that means you can get away with everything.'

'Shhhh,' said Mum. 'You're making too much noise!'

'How about *you* say *sorry*, munchkin,' said Patch, glaring at Lulu.

Lulu shook her head. 'No!'

Patch coughed. '*Scaredy-cat!*'

Lulu stood up. 'He called me *scaredy-cat!*' She stamped her foot.

'That's enough,' said Dad. 'Don't make a scene.'

Patch grunted. 'Ah, geez, we all know who the golden child is—'

'So Henry,' interrupted Mum. She nodded at his sundae. 'Is this your favourite part of today?'

'Uh-huh.' It *was* pretty awesome. Even a double scoop of gelato seemed sad and lonely next to this triple-whammy mountain range.

But later on, after they had finished eating, when Henry was crossing the road back to the holiday park and he was holding Dad's hand and the stars were coming out between the clouds, he couldn't help thinking it wasn't the winning or the three-scoop sundae or even discovering that he was a *genius* at noticing things that was the best part of the day.

It was the *surprising*.

Yes, that was the best thing ever. Everyone seeing him one way at the beginning of the day and then everyone suddenly seeing him differently at the end, his dad and Patch and all their friends and, now he was thinking about it, maybe even himself.

On his way back from the bathroom, Henry spotted the crimson dragster girl's bike parked outside the laundry. He peeked over the windowsill and watched the girl shoving clothes into a washing machine, even though it was so late.

'I can see you,' she said, without turning her head.

'No way,' said Henry.

'Yes way.' She tapped the glass on the front loader. 'You're in here.'

'Aaah!' said Henry and he felt a swell of gratitude that he was still wearing his shorts and a T-shirt and not his pyjamas. 'That's clever.'

'I bet you can't guess my full name,' said the girl,

turning round. 'What do you think Cassie might be short for?'

Henry shook his head. 'I'm not sure,' he said, hesitating. 'Cassata?'

'Ha! Too funny.'

'Cassava?'

'Nope!'

'I don't know,' said Henry. 'Cassandra?'

'Close. Good try.'

Henry laughed. 'Cassowary?'

'Do I look like a giant bird to you?'

'Casserole?'

'Tasty! But not even warm.'

Henry held up his hands in surrender. 'I give up.'

'Cassiopeia.'

'Gee.' Henry took a few steps forward, so he hovered in the doorway. 'Wow! That's a long name.'

Cassie turned and tocked some coins into the slot and spun some knobs on the washing machine. The clothes inside began to toss and swirl. 'Do you know where it comes from?' she asked. 'Cassiopeia?'

Henry fiddled with the seam of his T-shirt. 'Nope.'

'My mum named me after a bunch of stars, a big constellation,' said Cassie, popping her detergent into a laundry bag and zipping it up. 'Because at one time she wanted to be a big, big star.'

'And is she one?' Henry stepped right inside.

'Nah,' said Cassie. 'She sings on cruise ships now, which my Pop says are just floating RSLs. My mum reckons she left her run too late. And it's hard to be a big, big star when you've got a kid.'

'Oh,' said Henry.

'People call me Cassie because it's easier to say.'

'Which do you like better?' asked Henry.

'Cassie, I think. Because it's plain and everyday.'

'Okay, then,' said Henry. 'So I have a question too.' He cleared his throat.

Cassie tapped her foot. 'Sure!' she said. 'Ask away.'

'Well…' Henry tugged his ear. He rubbed his chin. 'How long… are you really staying down here?'

'Forever,' said Cassie.

Henry lifted his eyebrows. 'Forever?'

'I live here,' said Cassie. 'With my Pop.'

'In a tent?'

'No way!' Cassie rolled her eyes, as if she was beginning to suspect Henry was slower than she first thought. 'In a caravan!'

'In a caravan?' Henry blushed. 'Oh, yeah… right… I know… I mean… I just…'

'The one with the three meerkats staring out from the front window, just over the road from the amenities block and the dumpster.'

'Meerkats?' said Henry. 'Holy Flamoley.'

'Not real ones.'

'Oh.'

'Stuffed toys,' said Cassie, grinning. 'How's your bike? Haven't seen you ride it yet.'

'Well,' said Henry. 'It's okay – sort of. It's kind of…the tyres…well, hard to – it's got a bit of a problem…the brakes, you know…' The moths in his chest buzzed.

'You're funny,' said Cassie.

'I'm staying in the green tent,' said Henry, nodding his head, keen to change the topic. 'That one up there in the middle. Not far from the bikies.'

'I know,' said Cassie. 'You're with the big crowd.'

'Well,' said Henry. 'We're not *that* big!'

'Yeah, probably not. It's just my Pop goes to bed early every night, in a grump, because he reckons he can't sleep when there are so many little kids screeching about on their bikes in the park and so many loosey-goosey tarps flapping like sails in the wind. He sometimes has to get up before dawn, my Pop, because in the summer he works as a deckhand on a fishing charter boat and they need to get over the bar before the swell picks up. He's not too fond of tourists.' Cassie swung her laundry bag over her shoulder. 'But I like them,' she added. 'So there, Henry.'

'Hey! You remembered my name!'

'I've got a good memory,' she said, nodding.

'I was named after my great-grandfather who was an admiral in the navy.'

'So I'm a girl from the sky and you're a boy from the sea!'

'Ha!' said Henry. 'Yes. I like that.'

'You know, if you want,' said Cassie, 'maybe I can introduce you to my stingray?'

'Is that stuffed too?' asked Henry.

Cassie laughed, squinting. 'No, he's the real deal.'

Henry thought about the poisonous barb in a stingray's tail. 'I don't know,' he said. 'Aren't they kind of...dangerous?'

'Nahh,' said Cassie, sliding past him, her thongs flopping. She grabbed her bike and climbed on. 'Not this one. He's lost most of his tail, so he's completely harmless and super friendly. If you like, I can take you on a bike ride tomorrow and show you all sorts of interesting stuff.'

'Maybe we could go for a walk instead,' said Henry. 'Until my bike gets – fixed?'

'Well,' said Cassie, wrinkling her nose. 'We won't see as much.'

Just then Reed turned the corner, a towel wrapped around his neck. He popped his toothbrush out of his mouth.

'I've got to choof,' said Cassie, pushing off with one foot. 'But maybe I'll catch you later?' She glanced at Henry over her shoulder.

'Maybe,' said Henry, shrugging, suddenly awkward.

'See ya!' she called, riding off down the path, swerving around Reed.

'Whoah-ho!' Reed swaggered towards him. 'Whooo-hoo, Hennie! Girlfriend!'

'Shut up,' said Henry, glaring at him. 'You don't know anything.'

'She sure is a whizz on that bike!' said Reed, sauntering past. 'Maybe some kind of genius. Maybe you should ask your dad to put your training wheels back on, baby cheeks, so you can keep up with her?'

'And how many big fish have you caught so far?' called Henry. 'How many kingfish, hey?'

Reed saluted Henry with his toothbrush. 'None yet,' he cried, without looking back. 'But I will!'

Henry clomped off down the path. It was true! Reed Barone was the most irritating boy in the world, maybe even in the universe. The minute Henry was near him, he got itchy all over and started sprouting mean thoughts.

'Hey there, Heno.' Dad came zooming up the road on Patch's skateboard. 'I've been sent out on patrol. You admiring the view?'

Henry shook his head.

'You okay?'

Henry gazed at his dad for a moment, weighing up whether he should say something about Reed. But then he would also have to talk about the crimson dragster girl. And, oh blimey, that tiny

82

little story he had just told about his new bike being broken.

'Yes,' he said. 'I'm fine.'

'Check out this fog,' said Dad, gazing up. It was starting to slide across the sky like a long slow misty sigh. 'Isn't it astonishing, hey?' He flipped his board around. 'Race you home, genius boy!'

Henry charged after Dad down the road, running fast past the cabins with their flickering blue windows and the tinny sound of laughter, past the big bikie with the steel-wool beard, playing a noisy game of Celebrity Head with his bikie mates in the barbecue gazebo. He clambered over the lumpy roots of the pine trees and raced up to their tent, glowing like a Chinese lantern.

'Beat you, Dad!' he cried, as he zipped open the fly and crawled inside. He flopped down onto his Therm-a-Rest, panting. He peered up at the snug dome roof, the thin skin walls breathing in and out.

It struck Henry that the world was a little bit like a bag of mixed lollies: always full of some kind of surprise, some of them good, like clinkers and strawberry creams, and some of them horrible, like blue gummy cats and any orange lolly. Every day a jumbly rumbly bag of best moments and bad moments, joggled up tight together.

MAKiNG PLANS

'I did it!' crowed Lulu. She ran from the midday sunshine into the shade of the tarp. 'I DID IT! I swam in the deep this morning, in the pool, with my head under water, nearly the WHOLE way!'

Mum came puffing up to the tarp, juggling beach bags, hats, wet towels, floaties and an empty coffee cup.

'Tell them!' said Lulu, tugging at her red ruffled swimsuit.

'She did.' Mum dumped her load onto the table. 'She swam across the deep, with her head underwater the whole time. With no help at all.'

'Where's Reed?' asked Lulu. 'Because I need to tell him, RIGHT NOW!'

Dylan slid out a meat pie from a paper bag.

'He's over on the inlet side with my dad and Kale, trying his luck under the bridge.'

'Ha!' said Lulu. 'I bet he won't catch a single fish.'

'Now, Lulu, that's not nice talking,' said Mum. She slung the wet towels on a rack in the sun.

Lulu crossed her arms. 'Well, he said I'd have to swim in the hot wee-wee baby pool with Kale FOREVER but he was WRONG!'

'Guess what?' Dylan took a bite out of his pie.

'What?' asked Lulu, leaning on the table and kicking up her legs.

'I did three new skateboard tricks on the ramp today,' said Dylan, running his tongue along his teeth. 'A Casper Slide, a McTwist and a Nuclear Grab.'

'Whoooooooo,' said Lulu.

'I know,' said Dylan. 'Amazing, hey.' And he hoed into the rest of his pie with gusto.

'Yeah, so!' said Carey, spreading Nutella like thick icing on a slice of white bread. 'I just finished *The Calvin and Hobbes Tenth Anniversary Book*. And it was soooo good. You know my favourite bit? It's when Calvin becomes Spaceman Spiff, interplanetary explorer extraordinaire, because the aliens are always his mum or dad or his teacher Miss Wormwood! Don't you think that's so funny? It kills me, it really does.'

'Soon I'll be reading books all on my ownsome,' said Lulu. 'When I go to big school. And I will know all the words.'

Carey cut his slice of bread into four neat squares. 'You will,' he said. 'And you'll also learn how to count, tell news and tie your shoelaces—'

'I already can count to one hundred and tie my shoelaces. So there!'

'Oh, okay,' said Carey, with surprise. 'Well, that's good. I couldn't really tie my shoelaces properly till last year but I always had shoes with velcro to make it easier.'

'But I can't count to one hundred by twos yet,' said Lulu. 'So maybe they won't let me in? My friend Leonard Finkler can count to one hundred by twos and write his whole name, even the last one. The surname.'

Dylan wiped his mouth on the back of his hand. 'That's why you go to school, Lulu, so they can teach you that stuff.'

'Leonard Finkler is very smart,' said Lulu. 'He can play the violin and speak in French and make real custard and climb a rope all the way to the roof on his ownsome.' Lulu swooshed her hair away from her face.

'All at the same time?' asked Dylan.

'No, you big silly!' Lulu blew a raspberry.

'Yeah, well,' said Carey, 'my favourite thing about kindergarten was Friday Friendship because then you got free time and you could do what you wanted and take off your shoes, and even play computer—'

'It's your turn now, Heno,' interrupted Lulu.

'My turn?' asked Henry, pouring himself a bowl of Froot Loops. He sploshed the milk into the bowl, spilling just a little bit. 'What do you mean?'

Lulu's eyes glistened. 'Your bike! You know. And then Reed—'

'Oh, Lulu,' said Henry.

'What?' asked Lulu, lifting her hands.

Just then Dad pulled up in the car, with a jerk. He leapt out. 'Can someone grab the first-aid kit?' he called, slamming his door. He ran round to the passenger side.

'What's wrong?' cried Mum. She snatched the first aid kit from the top of the camp fridge.

'It's Patch,' said Dad. 'He got dumped.'

Patch got out of the car gingerly, a bloodied towel held up to his nose. He trudged over to a seat at the table. Mum poured some water from the kettle into a plastic bowl and grabbed a wad of serviettes.

'Okay,' said Dad. 'Now take the towel away.'

'Oh, gewwsh! Whoah!' said Dylan, gripping his stomach. 'That just put me off my pie.'

'Sorry, dude,' said Patch, with a laugh. 'I'll eat the rest for you in a sec.'

Dad dabbed at Patch's nose. 'Oh, phew,' he said. 'It's just a flesh wound. A tiny nick, really. My word, the way it bled, I was kind of expecting a hole where your nose used to be.'

'Ah, thanks, Dad,' said Patch.

'Were you bleeding in the water?' asked Henry, suddenly anxious.

'Well, yeah, at first,' said Patch. 'But don't worry, I kept an eye out for Jaws.'

'Ah, Heno,' said Dad, gazing at Henry. 'What will we do with you, son of my heart?'

'He's just troubleshooting.' Mum bent to stare at Patch's nose. 'Somebody in the family has to.'

'What are you saying?' asked Dad, with a grin.

'I send the kids out with you intact,' said Mum. 'And you always bring them back *maimed*!'

'Aw, now, come on! *Maimed*? Always?'

'Nearly always!'

Dad laughed. 'Noooooo-oooo,' he said, shaking his head in mock disbelief.

'What about the time when Patch was seven and rode his bike down that hill of death, with no brakes, through the turnstiles at the bottom, skidding right off near the bridge? I was picking gravel out of his rash for weeks.'

'Well, there was that,' said Dad.

'And the time Henry hammered his toenail off because you forgot to keep an eye on your tools while you were building the cubby?'

'Sometimes an adventurous life gets messy,' said Dad, hands on hips.

'Exactly! But it's always when they're with *you*.

Now hold still!' Mum stooped to place a puff of cotton wool over the graze on Patch's nose and stuck it down with a band-aid.

'Aw, not a band-aid,' groaned Patch. 'I'll look like a numpty.'

'No, you look like a cute little unicorn pony.' Lulu stared at the large bulge on Patch's nose.

'Aw, dog-goggles! Save me from all ponies,' said Patch. 'Deliver me from evil, please!' He glanced over at Dylan's pie. 'You finished with that?'

'Sure,' said Dylan, holding a hand against his stomach. He slid the paper bag down the table.

Patch snatched it up and wolfed the last bit down in two quick bites. 'Aaaah, that was great. I'm so famished. Any more where that came from?'

'Yep,' said Dylan, sliding a white paper bag over. 'You can have my sausage roll as well. I don't want it now.'

'You know what?' said Carey, wiping Nutella from the corners of his mouth with a serviette. 'I think surfing is dangerous. I think you'd be better off spending time in the tent, where it's nice and safe, reading all about Spaceman Spiff.'

'Ah, but you know what?' said Patch. 'I stood up on my board. On only my tenth go! Can you believe it? And the wave was as high as a cliff and quicksilver beneath my feet and just for a second, the dip down, I'm telling ya, it was like flying.'

'That's what it's like on the skate ramp too,' said Dylan.

'I know,' said Patch. 'But I haven't felt that way since I rode my bike down the hill of death!' He nodded at Henry and grinned.

The hill of death. Henry swallowed. His stomach panged. Lulu's words echoed in his ears. *It's your turn now.*

It was his turn now, his turn to be a daredevil. Everyone was waiting for him to ride his silver bike, to make a plan and to do it, snippety-snack, just like that! But *the hill of death.* Gosh, he would never do something that dumb, not even for a zillion billion dollars!

Henry rested on his parents' side of the tent, on their airbed, playing quietly with his *Star Wars* Lego figurines. Mum popped her head inside. 'Heno,' she whispered, 'a girl called Cassie is here to see you.'

'A *girl,*' said Patch, looking up from his phone. He rolled over onto his back. 'Whoaah-ho! Fast mover.' He gave Henry a nudge.

'Shhh, you!' Mum waved a finger.

Henry leapt up from the airbed. He slipped the Lego figurines into the tent pocket, then smoothed down his hair. When he came outside, he found Lulu talking to Cassie.

'Look…look…these are my favourites, these three,' she said, lining up the ponies on the table. 'This is Peony that you saved from terrible doom! And this is Marigold and Violet. But I have lots of others. See, this one is Bluebell but she is quite greedy and ate too many apples and got sick and spent a lot of time in hospital and now, here, she has lost half the hair from her tail. This green one is Clover. One time, she was galloping and fell out the car window accidentally and got run over by a truck. That's why she's a bit flat and not so fast anymore. This one is Poppy and this one is Tulip and this one is Primrose. Primrose is bossy and always telling the others what to do. She thinks she is the most beautiful pony in the world, just because her tail is rainbow glitter. She is always telling the other ponies that they are not as beautiful as her and they don't like to hear it.'

'I guess they wouldn't,' said Cassie.

'Do you think this one is pretty?' asked Lulu.

'Well—' said Cassie, smiling.

'Or do you think her eyes are wonky?' Lulu whispered. She held Clover up for inspection.

Cassie stared closely at the green pony. 'Maybe.'

'That's what I think! And the other ponies say so too,' said Lulu, nodding her head sadly. 'Even though I tell them not to mention it!'

'It's a problem alright,' said Mum. 'Now, let's not

take up all of Cassie's time, because she's come here
to say hello to Henry.'

'Hello,' said Henry. He stood awkwardly by the
camp fridge. His hands dangled like lumpy puffer
fish.

'Hello,' said Cassie, smiling at him. 'I told you I'd
see you round.'

'Yes,' said Henry. 'You did say that.'

'How's your bike?' she asked. 'Is it fixed yet?'

'Fixed?' Dad looked up from the table, where he
was chopping parsley.

'Aaaaaah,' said Henry.

'The brakes?' asked Cassie.

A bunch of newborn moths rose up in his chest.
Henry snatched a breath of warm, muggy air.

Dad lifted an eyebrow. 'The brakes?'

'Yeah…well…ah—' Henry cleared his throat.

Dad put down his knife. 'Hey there,
now…Heno…'

'Because I've got some fish scraps for Heathcliff,'
said Cassie. 'And I thought we could ride round to
the wharf to drop them off.' She tugged at the straps
of her floral backpack.

Lulu stopped nibbling the ear of her green pony.
She placed Clover carefully next to Violet. 'Who's
Heathcliff?'

'He's an old stingray,' said Cassie, hopping off
her bike and leaning it against the table. 'I bring him

92

fish scraps every afternoon, down by the wharf.'

Dad looked over at Cassie. 'Heathcliff? Now that's an unusual name for a stingray.'

'My mum is a singer on the cruise ships,' said Cassie. 'And one of her best, hardest songs is about a boy called Heathcliff and a girl called Cathy. It's got very high notes. She can almost crack the wine glasses when she sings it.'

'Aah, I see,' said Dad. '"Wuthering Heights" by Kate Bush. That explains it!'

'That's it,' nodded Cassie.

'So...Heathcliff – is he...safe?' asked Mum.

'Oh yes,' said Cassie. 'He lost most of his tail a long time ago. No one knows exactly how. Maybe it was a fishing accident. But he doesn't have a barb, so he's very safe. He's a bit of a sook, really. That's what my Pop reckons.'

'Can I come?' asked Lulu.

'No,' said Henry, quickly.

'It's not fair,' said Lulu. 'I never get to do anything fun.'

'Never?' asked Dad.

'NEVER!' said Lulu. She snatched up Peony and stomped off into the tent.

'Gosh, she's a bit overtired,' said Mum, with an apologetic grimace. 'Sorry.'

'That's okay,' said Cassie. 'So do you want to come?' She tilted her head, waiting for Henry's answer. 'Don't worry! I always feed Heathcliff down by the table where they gut the fish in the shallows. So it's not deep.'

Henry bit his top lip and blinked furiously, as if a spotlight was shining suddenly and he could barely see. Cassie gazed around the campsite and over towards the trailer. She nodded at Henry. 'Is that your bike under there?'

A shiver prickled down Henry's spine. The bike was locked up tight to the trailer, covered in a tarp to keep it from rusting. But even so the front wheel was peeking out, like a nosy uninvited guest. Something stuck hard in Henry's throat.

'What's wrong with the brakes?' asked Cassie.

'Well,' said Dad. 'The thing is, Cassie, that…um—'

Henry was hot and cold at the same time and everything was beginning to be edged in grey fur. 'Dad,' he murmured.

Mum opened her eyes wide. 'Daniel,' she said. She pursed her lips tight.

'I'll go with you!' Reed burst out of his tent like a jack-in-the-box. 'I'd love to get up close and personal to an old stingray.' He stood there, smirking his usual cheesy, smartypants grin. 'I'll get my bike.'

Cassie glanced at Henry. 'Well—'

'NO!' It came out like a loud bark. A lick of hot anger curled right through Henry. He glared at greedy-guts Reed, wishing his eyes were fierce laser points so he could wither him up on the spot like a dry brown leaf. 'You can't come!' he hissed.

'You can't stop me!' said Reed. His whole face flushed a dark cherry red.

Dad coughed. 'Now, boys.'

Reed shoved a fist into the pocket of his shorts. He glared at Cassie. 'If you want to ride with Hennie,' he said, with a sneer, 'you'd better get ready to wait for eternity because he—'

'SHUT UP,' said Henry, lunging forward. He snatched up Lulu's battered green pony from the table and chucked it hard at Reed's head.

Reed ducked and the pony bounced off the side of the tent and plopped straight into a red bucket. 'Whoops! You missed!' said Reed, with a snigger. 'Except now you've done it! Because that pony is swimming in my bait bucket and it's going to stink of squid. Hope you're okay about breaking the bad news to Lulu?'

'Okay, Reed, big fella,' said Dad, standing up. 'I think that's enough. How about you go check on the older boys in the rec room and tell them we're just about to get the World Cup cricket match started?'

Reed sniffed. 'Sure thing, Mr Hoobler.' He shot Henry a sneaky side-glance. 'I might take my *bike* though,' he said. 'Because it'll be faster than walking.'

'Thanks mate, you do that,' said Dad, with a sigh.

He strode over to the Barones' tent and fished the battered green pony out of the bait bucket. 'I'll just go and give Clover a wash at the sink,' he whispered, holding the dripping pony by her tail. He snatched the pump soap from the top of the camp fridge.

Henry gazed at his mum in despair. He felt hollowed out, like a bushfire had raged through him. Why did he let Reed Barone get under his skin? Why couldn't he think of something smartypants funny to say? Why did all his words get bottled up in the back of his throat? Now Cassie would be thinking he was some kind of crazy hot-head kid and she would never want to spend any time with him again.

Mum shook out a tea towel. 'Are you staying around here, Cassie?'

'Well, I live here,' said Cassie, nodding. 'With my Pop. In the caravan with the meerkats behind the fancy cabins, near the toilet block.'

'Oh, wow,' said Mum. 'Not real meerkats?'

'No,' said Cassie, smiling. 'Just funny stuffed ones. But my Pop reckons they put thieves off. They've got very beady eyes, and at night they sure look like the real thing.'

'Beady eyes!' said Mum. 'I love it!'

'I used to live with my Nan too,' said Cassie. 'But she got sick and died last year. Her liver stopped working.'

'Oh, Cassie,' said Mum, dropping her tea towel.

Cassie nodded. 'It happened quick.'

'That's terrible. I'm so sorry to hear that!'

'Nan and Pop had been married for fifty-nine years and three hundred and fifty days!'

'Oh, so close to sixty!' Mum cried, her eyes shiny. 'Such a long time.'

'Yes,' said Cassie, swivelling her bike bell. 'But the strangest thing is the day after Nan died, Pop packed up all her clothes and took them to the op shop, just like that. I don't know what made him do that. Maybe he was too sad to see Nan's slippers poking out from underneath the bed, like they were waiting for her to come back any minute.' She looked up and shrugged.

'Yes,' said Mum, nodding. 'Yes. Perhaps that's it. Everyone has a different way of being sad.'

'But I went up to the shop later and bought her pink dressing-gown back with my own pocket money, and when I go to bed at night I hug it up close because it still smells just like her. Like Crabtree and Evelyn. Like roses.' Cassie's golden eyes were sheeny. She sniffed and tapped her bike bell. 'You know,' she said, flicking a straggly curl over her shoulder, 'I'm pretty good at cricket.'

'I bet you are,' said Mum.

'My Pop almost played for Australia.'

'Really!'

Cassie nodded. 'So I can bowl a pretty mean googly!'

Dad plodded back from the gazebo, carrying the sodden pony out in front. 'Hope that does the trick,' he said. He pegged it up on the clothing rack.

'Cassie can bowl a pretty mean googly,' said Mum, turning her head. 'Her Pop almost played for Australia!'

'Woweeee,' said Dad, rubbing his hands together. 'Yes! A spin bowler. You sound like a lethal weapon!'

'Maybe,' said Cassie, with a grin.

'Well, would you like to do us a massive favour and give us a hand this arvo? I reckon the kids will need all the help they can get, taking on us mighty warriors.'

'Mighty warriors?' called Patch, from the tent. 'Peuuuwww! More like tarnished golden oldies.'

'Now, now,' said Dad. 'How about you show a little bit of respect in there?' He clutched his side. 'Although the old back is not what it was, that's for sure. So...what do you reckon, Cassie? You up for the big bash?' He slid the cutting board across the table and scraped a small mountain of parsley into a Tupperware container.

'I'd love to,' said Cassie. She turned and gazed at Henry directly. Her eyes lit up like the jasper stones on his Nonna's mantelpiece, her whole face glowing like she had been given an extraordinary prize, even though all they were going to do was play a dumb old game of cricket. 'Would it be alright if I just go and change my shoes and tell my Pop that I'm going to play?'

'No problem,' said Dad. 'Invite your Pop along too, if you want.'

'Ah, no,' said Cassie. 'He likes to have a nap in the arvo. He's pretty old, you know, practically ancient. He even has ear tufts.'

'Almost a caveman.' Dad touched his own ears.

'How about Heathcliff?' asked Mum.

'I'll feed him later. He won't mind.' Cassie turned to Henry. 'Maybe we can go for a ride another time?'

Henry's heart pounded in his ears.

'When your bike is—'

'Sure,' interrupted Henry, his voice cracking. 'Another time.' He shot a quick glance at his dad.

'That's one flash bike,' said Dad to Cassie. 'A dragster. I love it.'

'I know', said Cassie. 'It used to belong to my mum. My Pop fixed it up for me, like new.'

'Well, I'm sure it's going to be a heap of fun to ride around together,' said Dad. He pinched his chin and nodded at Henry. 'Another time. Now that sounds like a plan.'

WORLD CUP CRICKET

When it was Henry's turn to bat that afternoon, he ducked every ball, even the gentle, juicy, smashable ones. The other kids groaned in agony. 'Ohhh, nooooooo!'

'I told you we should have played him as twelfth man,' said Reed. 'Even Lulu could do better!'

Cassie ignored them all and kept clapping harder. She fluttered up and down the sidelines, calling out instructions. 'That's the way. Take your time, Henry. Get your eye in. Hold firm and play it forward, okay? And don't forget to move your feet! Straight down the wicket, yeah? You're doing well.'

When Henry smashed Mr Carson down the bike path for four on the very next ball, Cassie did three cartwheels in a row and cried out, 'Hello, Mr Cricket!

100

Did you see? Whoo-hooo! A lofted drive! Take a bow!'
And Henry laughed and bowed to her and to his dad
and to the rest of his team.

'Well done, Heno!' said Dad. 'That's the ticket.'

'Hey!' called Mr Barone from the sand flats.
'Just remember whose side you're on.'

Patch clapped. 'See, you can do it, Henry. You
just have to *focus*.'

Henry nodded. He cleared his throat. He licked
his lips. He clunked his bat against the bike path,
like a warrior, inviting the contest, welcoming it even.
The skin tingled on the back of his hands. As Mr
Carson bolted down the path, Henry lifted his bat
and shuffled forwards. But the ball came skimming
through so fast and low that he felt the breeze of it,
before he'd even spotted it. It smacked hard against
the boogie board wicket, flinging it sideways.

'Howzat!' cried Mr Carson, trotting backwards,
waving a finger in the air.

Reed rolled his eyes. 'Aw, geez, Henny. Clean
bowled! Typical.'

'Neeeeigh,' said Lulu to Reed. 'If you've got
nothing nice to say, you shouldn't say anything, Reed
Barone.'

'You should take your own advice, Lulu Poobler,'
said Reed.

Henry slunk back to the sideline, kicking at the
grass, suddenly angry and disappointed. Cassie patted

him on the shoulder. 'Ah, bummer,' she said. 'What a daisycutter! You know, that ball would have taken out anyone, even Donald Bradman, the very best batsman in the whole wide world!'

Henry sniffed. 'Really?' he said, slumping down on the grass.

'For sure! It was a hard-to-read ball,' said Cassie.

'Really?'

'Promise,' said Cassie. 'I swear on my Nan's Bible.' And for some reason, the way Cassie held Henry's gaze for a long moment, her golden eyes so clear and vivid, made the fuzzy ball of worry in his chest suddenly lift and float away.

When Cassie's turn came to bat, she belted the ball; hooking, pulling, sweeping and slogging, smashing it through the gaps, over the tents, out on the sand flats, down the bike path, in between the cabins. She dashed down the pitch with a leap, a skip and a fiery 'YES!' as she hunted down more and more runs with each of her batting partners, first Dylan, then Jay and finally Patch.

'I thought you said you were a bowler?' said Dad, scratching his head, after he had finally bowled Patch out.

'I can bat a bit,' said Cassie.

'A bit! Sheezy-wheezy. That might be the understatement of the century. You're a whirlwind. I've never had to run so much. Every single one of us

102

has shredded feet from chasing your shots through the reeds and I'm pretty sure I'm going to need to see a chiropractor tomorrow. I might even need traction!'

'Here we go! Drinks time,' said Mr Barone, carrying out a tray. He crouched down and placed it on the grass and then handed Dad a plastic cup. 'Pink lemonade. It's the closest thing we have to a sports drink. But it should do the trick. Get us back on track. Or at the very least send the kids hypo.'

Lulu pranced about on the grass. 'I LOVE pink lemonade,' she said. She scooped up a glass and took a long gulp and smiled, a rosy moustache stained across her top lip. 'Are we winning yet?'

'Not yet,' said Dylan. 'But we're on the way.'

'Haha,' said Patch, giving Dad a little shove in the back. 'You ready for your thrashing yet? No more excuses now. It's time to bat, old man.' He threw the ball to Cassie. 'You take the new ball, champ.'

'Nah,' said Cassie, smiling. 'You go first.' She tossed it back.

Patch rubbed the ball while he waited for Dad and Mrs Barone to take their positions. And then he charged down the pitch, hurling ball after ball like he was throwing lightning bolts. But even though he steamed in like an express train, bowling long-hops and yorkers, pounding the pitch with sledgehammer feet, only one wicket came his way.

When everyone had taken their turn to bowl – Dylan, Jay, Carey, Reed, Henry, even Lulu and Kale – and the runs were mounting and the adults were beginning to get lighthearted and giddy, sensing a win within their grasp, Dylan turned to Cassie and knelt before her. 'Help us, Obi-Wan Kenobi, you're our only hope.'

Cassie laughed. She tossed the ball up and down, up and down with one hand and then she reset the field, pointing at Dylan, Patch and Jay, bringing all of her big boy fielders up close to the strike end. 'It's best to cook your victims slowly,' she called with a big grin. 'That's what my Pop says.'

'Whomp! Them's fighting words,' cried Mr Barone. 'Bring it on!'

Four balls later, Cassie had two wickets. And two overs later the game was finished and the kids had won the first ever Yelonga World Camp Cricket Cup. The big boys bolted around the grass with their T-shirts flapped over their heads, singing 'Victory!' They slapped hands, swapped T-shirts and laughed and sang all the way to the bathroom to wash up for dinner.

The moon rose like a pale pearl.

Kale held Henry's hand as they walked back to the tent. He smiled at the painted walking figure on the bike path. 'Hello, man,' he said.

'That's not a man!' said Lulu. 'It's not even real, you silly!'

Dad limped in front. 'Egad, Cassie, you're a hypnotist!'

'A snake charmer, more like it,' said Mr Carson. 'Did you see the way the ball danced down the pitch? One second it was going one way and the next it was striking you on the pads.'

'How did you get so good?' asked Mum.

'She's some kind of genius,' said Mrs Barone. 'Like Heno at board games. Is that right?'

'Nope!' Cassie scrunched up her nose. 'Mostly I just got good because my Pop is always taking me down to the nets when he picks me up from school. We go there nearly every day, except for in the summer, when there's a lot of cricket to watch on telly instead.'

'Ah,' said Dad. 'So it's all practice!' He arched his eyebrows at Henry. 'Just practice, practice, practice.'

Henry shook his head. He turned to his mum. 'Can Cassie stay for dinner?'

'If she'd like to,' said Mum.

'Sure I would,' said Cassie.

'Do you need to go tell your Pop?' Mum touched Cassie gently on the shoulder.

'It's okay. He's gone to the bowling club now to play a little bit of bingo, so it's leftovers for me tonight.'

'Oh, right,' said Mum, glancing over at Dad.

Lulu tucked her hand through Cassie's arm.

'Maybe we can go for a walk to the park after dinner and have a go on the big nest swing and the pirate ship?'

'Maybe,' said Cassie. She gazed over at Henry. 'If you want to.'

'Sure,' said Henry, with a grin. 'Sounds good.'

After a quick World Cup Cricket presentation, where every kid was officially presented with a slightly tattered *You'll Always Belonga at Yelonga Inlet Haven* baseball cap, everyone tucked heartily into a World Cup Cricket potluck dinner. There were spicy chicken kebabs, tabouleh, tzatziki and flat bread, linguini marinara, cheesy macaroni, avocado and mango salad and for dessert, big bowls of fresh raspberries and cream, with crushed choc-chip cookies sprinkled on top. When the kids finished eating, they all washed and dried the dishes together, chasing each other around the gazebo sink, flicking each other's legs with tea towels.

Then everyone gathered round a small fire, toasting marshmallows and drinking hot chocolate. And Cassie told them stories about the boats she had seen shipwrecked out on the breakwater near the bar, and the sea rescues her Pop had been involved in. She told them about the fishing records her Pop had broken and all the rare species he had caught and thrown back: the elegant wrasse, the Ballina angelfish, eastern blue devilfish, and even one time a great white shark.

'A great white shark,' breathed Reed. 'He sounds like a fishing *genius*. I may need to meet this man.'

Cassie talked about her Nan and how she made the best rice pudding in the world, with a cinnamon and nutmeg skin on top and with real vanilla beans but not too sweet, and how her Nan had crocheted hand towels for the oyster festival to help raise money for the school library, even though she was sick with cancer and couldn't get out of bed.

Then Mum took Lulu, Henry and Cassie for a visit to the park. They played tag all over the pirate ship and then took turns spinning each other dizzy on the mini twister maypole. They hung from the monkey bars until their arms ached and they all agreed they never ever wanted to live in the jungle.

'It's nearly time to go,' said Mum.

'Not yet,' cried Lulu. 'We haven't even been on the nest swing!'

'Hop on,' said Mum. 'Because I'm ready to push.'

Mum pushed Henry, Cassie and Lulu on the big-netted swing. They gripped on tight as they flew up and down together, the world tilting this way and that, the damp rising against their backs. As the swing began to slow, they watched the moon make a wobbly lemon ladder out on the water.

'I wish this day could go on forever,' murmured Cassie.

'Me too,' breathed Henry.

'Me five,' said Lulu, with a sigh, hugging her ponies beneath the front of her hoodie.

After that, they walked slowly back to the tent, down past the wharf and the quiet bobbing fishing boats, along the bike path, counting the sea birds sleeping on the tops of the light poles.

When they got back to the tent, Cassie tucked Lulu into bed with all her ponies and kissed Peony without hesitation. And then Mum and Henry escorted Cassie back to her darkened caravan, with the three beady-eyed meerkats.

'Goodnight,' Cassie whispered, as she lifted the zipper to the annexe. 'Thank you for having me!' She turned around and doffed her new baseball cap.

'It was a pleasure, Cassie,' said Mum, smiling. 'We hope we see you tomorrow.'

'Me too!' said Cassie, flashing them a big grin.

Mum took Henry's hand.

They walked back towards the tent, over the speed humps, their thongs snick-snocking in time. A truck braked in the distance and then, a moment later, rumbled over the bridge. A bat flapped heavily above the tips of the pine trees.

Mum squeezed Henry's hand. 'Aaaaah,' she breathed. Their eyes met in the dimness.

'What?' Something caught in the back of Henry's throat. He squeezed her hand tight.

'Oh, it's just…' Mum brushed her face. 'Well, what a girl, hey!'

Henry nodded.

'She's plucky,' said Mum. 'Don't you think?'

'What does that mean?' asked Henry.

'Brave!' said Mum. 'And daring and gutsy.'

They were silent together. A cool night breeze lifted up the nearby tarps.

The sky was filled with stars, right down to the horizon, like Lulu had gone crazy with a glitter shaker.

'I think you should tell Cassie the truth,' said Mum. 'About your bike and the brakes—'

Henry pulled his hand away.

'Just tell her you're still learning how to ride.'

'I don't want to.'

'It's just so much better to be honest,' said Mum. 'Always. But especially with friends.'

'She'll think I'm a baby!'

'Oh, Henry.' Mum breathed in deep. 'I don't think so. She's different.'

Henry wanted to share something he had noticed about Cassie too. But finding the right words was hard. He scratched his head and thought for a moment. And then it came to him. What he wanted to say. But he couldn't say it out loud! Good gravy, what would Mum think? Maybe she'd think he was silly! Or in super-soppy over-the-top love! Then what if Reed found out? He would twist it in a second. In any case, how could Henry know such a thing about Cassie, in such a short time?

Mum delivered one of her sneaky catch-him-by-surprise kisses on the top of his head. 'I have a hunch,' she murmured, 'that Cassie is the type of friend who is as rare as hen's teeth.'

'Ha!' said Henry. He got what his mum meant straight away this time. He knew hens did not have teeth. 'So, unbelievably rare. Like almost extinct?'

'Yes. Exactly,' said Mum.

A warm slosh of happiness flooded through Henry. His mum could see the special thing in Cassie too. How Cassie was bright and loud and more alive than a normal person! And how she had the clever, funny knack of making everything seem possible.

But a second later, a sudden rush of bruising sadness rose up. Because Holy Lamoley! How could it be? Why did it work that way? How could he meet a friend as rare as a hen's tooth on a holiday, so far from home?

LOST

It was the middle of the night when Lulu woke him.

'Henry,' she whispered. A warm salty drop dripped down his cheek.

'It's okay,' he said, stretching sleepily out to rub her head. 'It's just a bad dream.'

'He-enry,' she said, with a small sniff.

He opened his eyes. The tent was dark. Sleep tugged again. It wanted to wrap and roll him up.

Lulu shook his shoulder. 'Hen-ry!' He heard the small hiccup in her breath. It was the sound she only made when she was in trouble and had been crying and was sure the world was about to end.

'What's wrong?' Henry stretched his eyes open.

'It's Clover,' said Lulu.

'What?' Henry rolled onto his side. He could

see the shadowy outline of Lulu's head.

'It's my pony. She's gone,' said Lulu, sniffing.
'I think I left her at the park.'

'Oh,' said Henry. 'That's no good.'

Lulu started to sob quietly.

'Did you tell Dad?'

'And Mum,' whispered Lulu. 'But they both said I have to wait until morning.' She wriggled over and buried her head in the hollow of Henry's neck, her breath like a hot mist. She flung her arm across his chest.

Henry stroked her head, smoothing her sweaty fringe back. 'It's okay,' he said. 'It'll be okay.'

'But Clover has already fallen out of the car before and got run over by a truck,' said Lulu, shuddering. 'And already she is worried she's not my favourite and now she will be thinking she is like Gretel and I've left her out in the woods, except she doesn't have any breadcrumbs and no clever Hansel and she is flat now anyway and not so fast. And what if someone comes in the morning to tidy up the park and throws her in the bin because they think she is rubbish and then the bin truck comes and takes her away before I can get there? And I've been a mean mother because I only love my pretty horses! That's why she got left behind and now she will be taken away and I will be sad forever.'

'Oh, Lulu,' said Henry.

'I know,' said Lulu.

Henry thought about the battered, crooked-eyed green pony, lying somewhere out on the grass, soaking wet with dew and bewilderment, wondering why she had been left behind.

'Maybe a pelichicken will dive down and scoop her up for a late-night snack.' Lulu gave a heave and a double sniff.

'I don't think pelicans like to snack on plastic ponies. Especially green ones that smell like apple.'

'She doesn't smell so much like apple anymore,' said Lulu. 'Not since she fell in the bait bucket.'

'Oh, Lulu,' said Henry. 'I'm sorry. It was an accident.'

'I know, but maybe a feral cat might get her now,' said Lulu. 'Or a fox or a wild boar!'

'I don't think there are any wild boars about.'

'But there are feral cats!' said Lulu. 'And foxes! Aren't there?'

Henry breathed in deep. He didn't want to think about that.

'What about water rats?' asked Lulu. 'They might drag Clover back to their burrow and make a nest in her mane and then let their naughty little rat babies nibble at her hooves and she will be all eaten up.'

Henry knew what Cassie would do. She wouldn't let a fox or a wild boar or a feral cat or even nasty mane-loving, hoof-nibbling rodents stop her from venturing out into the dark and helping Lulu.

It struck Henry that perhaps he was waiting for the *exact right moment* to be daring and brave. The exact right moment when he felt no worry at all, not one tiny flicker. But what if that moment never came? He might end up being ancient, with tufts of hair bursting out of his ears and never moving off the lounge. Maybe he'd end up spending his whole life watching telly and clapping his hands at the daring, plucky people on the screen.

But now he was thinking about it, perhaps the bravest people were the ones who were a little bit worried or scared the whole time and did brave things anyway? Maybe they were more truly brave than people who did daring things without a second thought? And then he remembered what Mum said about the fluttering moth inside her chest, the sense of dread and how important it was to give that feeling a little bit of room and say, 'Aaaah, there you are!'

'Aaaaah, there you are!' whispered Henry.

'What?' said Lulu.

Henry tapped a hand against his chest. 'But it's not the whole story,' he breathed.

'What?' said Lulu. 'I don't get it. What's not the whole story?'

'Nothing.' Henry shook his head. 'Don't worry.' He took a deep breath. Something tocked in the middle of his chest, firm as the satisfying chink of

114

a coin in his purple pig moneybox. He was resolved, even though he was scared. He wriggled out of his sleeping-bag, shedding it like a skin.

'Where are you going?' asked Lulu, sitting up.

Patch rolled over in his sleep, giving a little groan and a shiver. His leg sprawled out, nudging Henry's ankle.

'Shhhhh,' said Henry, leaning down. He pressed his hand against Lulu's mouth. 'We're going to rescue Clover.'

'Now?' murmured Lulu. 'Right this minute?'

'Exactly!'

Lulu grabbed Henry's hand and kissed it with great, moist extravagance. 'Thank you!' she breathed. 'Oh, thank you, Henry!'

The sky was black and a cool wind blew in from the ocean. Henry shivered in his pyjamas. He clutched his lantern and Lulu's hand tightly as they hurried between the tents, treading carefully to avoid twanging the tent ropes.

'Are you going to turn the light on yet?' whispered Lulu.

'In a little while,' murmured Henry, squeezing Lulu's hand. 'Not yet. Not until we get to the park. Because it's very dark there and we're going to need it, if we're going to find Clover.'

Lulu gazed up. 'What has happened to all the stars?'

'Behind the clouds,' said Henry, concentrating on his feet.

'And the moon?' asked Lulu.

Henry squeezed her hand again. 'Same place.'

'Oh, no, Henry,' breathed Lulu. 'I wish they weren't all swallowed up.'

'Me too,' said Henry. He wanted the moon to come out very badly. He longed for a crisp silver moon, dangling in the sky like a Christmas bauble. As they tiptoed past a darkened tent, it rumbled with loud gurgles and snorts. They stopped dead still.

'Gosh!' gasped Lulu. 'What is that?'

It sounded like a dragon. Like a huge, slumbering dragon guarding a cave full of treasure.

Henry dug his bare feet into the grass. Cold dirt rose between his toes. He was not going to think about dragons. He was not going to think about their greedy eyes and their cold, cold scales and their flickering lizard tongues. Or the way they liked to eat up and spit out the bones of little children. Besides, there was surely a sensible answer for nearly everything, if only he could remember to think hard enough.

'What *is* it?' asked Lulu, drawing near.

He listened carefully. The noise was not just coming from one tent. It was coming from a ring of tents all around them. An image sharpened in his mind. 'Aaaah,' he whispered. 'It's snoring!' He wanted to giggle out loud. Maybe it was the big bikie with the steel-wool beard? How funny and strange to be so close to big people he didn't know, listening to their night noises.

Another loud honk blared out. A tiny plume of embarrassment billowed in Henry. Big bikies were snoozing in their tents right next to him, somehow fragile and weak as babies. Something warm and achy clenched tight in his chest.

'I don't think so,' said Lulu.

'You don't think what?'

'That does *not* sound like snoring to me, Henry.'

'It doesn't?'

'No!' Lulu sloped in on Henry, almost tripping over his foot. 'Henry,' she whispered impatiently, 'that is the sound of werewolves.'

'Werewolves?'

Another great snorkeling gargling splutter came from the tent behind them, then a long drawn out strangled breath.

'There's no such thing as werewolves.' Henry's feet were dripping with dew and strands of grass.

'Oh, Henry,' said Lulu, with a deep, patient weariness.

Henry turned his head and listened closely to the gurgling and the gargling, the murmuring and the

117

muttering, the snickering and the snuckering coming directly from the tent beside them. It sounded like something or someone was slowly being smothered. The hair on the back of Henry's neck prickled.

'Do you think that person is in the middle of turning into a werewolf or turning back?' asked Lulu.

'Let's go,' said Henry, marching forward and dragging Lulu with him.

'Because Leonard Finkler says the only way to kill a werewolf is with a silver bullet.'

Henry took a deep breath. They were nearly at the end of the tents. Maybe they should cut across to the bike path and follow that up past the wharf and then round to the park? Whatever they did, they shouldn't run, just in case. Maybe that would be an invitation for a chase, the way it was with dogs.

'The main way you get turned into a werewolf is if you get bitten and the saliva of a werewolf enters your blood,' whispered Lulu. 'But Leonard Finkler told me that if you drink the water out of a footprint of a werewolf, that can do it too.'

'Gosh, this Leonard Finkler. He knows an awful lot,' muttered Henry.

'Yes,' said Lulu. 'He might be a genius.'

'He sure is something!' said Henry.

'But there's no moon tonight,' said Lulu, 'so maybe they will just stay inside. I don't think werewolves like to eat without the moon.'

'Well, that's great!' Henry gazed up at the sky. Now he would need to pray the moon didn't come out at all.

'Leonard Finkler says the seventh son is always a werewolf,' said Lulu. 'And that in some countries, families would leave their seventh son out on a hill in the middle of the night or have them adopted. What does *adopted* mean, Henry?'

'Oh, *enough*,' hissed Henry. 'Enough already.'

They strode past another dark tent, shaped like the big top of a circus, with two flags flapping fiercely at the peak. A breathy, throttling sputter came from deep inside. 'Snooooork euuuuurgle yeooooooooowl!'

'Henry!' whispered Lulu, hugging his arm frantically.

Henry was sure he could feel the hot snuffling breath of something against the backs of his knees. He imagined the flash of teeth, the snarl, the claws sharp as knives and the glowing eyes.

'Run!' he gasped.

And they both turned and bolted through a gap between the tents.

FOUND

Henry and Lulu didn't stop running until they drew near to the darkened indoor swimming pool. Henry bent over a wooden fence to catch his breath. The soles of his feet stung. 'Oooh,' he groaned. 'Aww, no!' He smacked the wooden post.

'What?' asked Lulu, panting. 'What's wrong, Henry?'

'I dropped the lantern,' said Henry. He clapped his hands to his face and let them slide down, gazing at Lulu hopelessly.

'Oh, Henry!' said Lulu.

A lone bird gave a low mournful cry out on the water. The estuary lights flashed red, then green. A sweep of white light grazed the top of the hill, from the distant lighthouse out at sea. They listened to the tide splash in, tumbling like a bubbling stream over the breakwater.

'Maybe we should go back?' said Lulu. 'And get up early in the morning?'

A hard, burning rock rose up in Henry's throat. He thought longingly of his bed, the warmth of his sleeping-bag, the quiet, reassuring sound of Patch's slow and steady breathing. Then he thought about the battered, stinky squid pony, who was lost, and Cassie, who was daring and gutsy and brave. He ran a hand over his face. 'No,' he whispered. 'No. But no more talking about you-know-whats!' He took her hand. 'Okay?'

'Okay, Henry,' said Lulu.

'And I think when you go to big school, you should try to make some new friends.'

'Why?' asked Lulu.

'Because I think Leonard Finkler might not be so healthy for you!'

'But he does know an awful lot about you-know-whats,' said Lulu.

'Yes,' said Henry. 'That's what I mean.'

'But not as much as he knows about zombies!'

'*Lulu!*'

'What?'

'*Enough!*'

They traipsed silently past the fishing charter boats chafing against the wharf. Henry thought about all the creatures beneath the water – gropers, jellyfish, seahorses, grey nurse sharks, plankton, octopi, starfish and an old stingray called Heathcliff.

Birds rustled on the tops of the light poles, peering down at them. Henry had never felt so grateful for so many warm pools of streetlight in his whole life. The birds shook their heads and ducked their beaks back behind their wings. Gosh, there was so much going on in the world! Up in the sky and out on the sea and beneath the sea and on the earth and below the earth. It was a lot to take in.

Lulu itched her nose. 'What about Jesus?'

'What about him?'

'He came back from the dead,' said Lulu. 'And so—'

'And so what?'

'Well, do you think that makes him a z—'

'STOP!'

Henry didn't know a lot about Jesus, only the stories Mrs Harradence, his Scripture teacher, taught them in class on Wednesday afternoons when they were all tired out from playing soccer at lunch. But the thing he did know was that when Jesus came back from the dead it was to save people, not hunt them down.

'What about ghosts, Henry?' said Lulu. 'Do you think they're real?'

Holy Yamoley! The scariest thing about this trip

122

was Lulu! He'd have been better off searching for Clover on his own. If Lulu kept at it, he might have a heart attack. Was it possible to have a heart attack at his age? What was that noise in his ears? Was that his heart thudding? Maybe his heart had got detached from its rightful place and was roving around his body like a rogue satellite.

'Do you know what I'm scared about?' asked Lulu.

Henry sighed. He shook his head. 'Nope.' He wasn't sure he wanted to know, either. He seriously doubted whether Lulu was really scared of anything. When it came down to it, Lulu might be the next bravest person he knew, after Cassie. Who else could decide to swim across the deep end and do it only a few days later?

'I'm scared about going to school,' she said, sniffing.

Henry stopped walking. He turned to gaze at her. The water swooshed in the distance. 'You're scared about going to school?'

Lulu looked up at him. 'Yes.' A breeze ruffled her fringe.

'Oh.' He was suddenly aware of the sticky smallness of Lulu's hand, the lightness of her bones.

'What if nobody likes me and my new teacher is a meanie with frizzy hair,' said Lulu, 'and I am in a different class from Leonard Finkler and he makes a lot of friends, maybe a zillion billion and they're all boys and they ask him to play soccer with them every day and they tell him he has to choose and he shouts at me to go away in the playground and I don't know where to go and I have no ponies to talk to because I'm not allowed to take them to school, not even a single one, and what if I get tired of spelling and reading and telling news and I want to lie down? Or what if I can't get my new lunchbox open and all the other girls laugh at me? Or I accidentally wet my pants and then get stuck down the toilet and nobody notices? What if I turn my library book from the bottom and tear the page and the librarian sends me to the storeroom and locks me up and forgets I'm there and leaves me in there for the whole entire weekend? What if I'm lonely, Henry? Oh, what if I'm lonely? I think I need to stay home for one more year, I do!'

'Oh, Lulu,' said Henry. 'If you get lost, I'll come and find you. And if you're lonely, I'll hug you better. I'll look after you, Lulu, don't worry.'

'Truly ruly?'

'Cross my heart,' said Henry. 'And even if Leonard Finkler is not in your class, you will be okay.'

'How do you know?'

'Well, because you're funny.' Henry snuck a sneaky catch-her-by-surprise kiss on the top of Lulu's head. 'And clever and adorable and you're going to make lots and lots and lots of friends.'

Lulu flung her arms around his waist and squinched him tight, for ages and ages, until all Henry could smell was her apple shampoo.

'Come on,' he whispered finally. 'Let's go.' They tramped up the path, holding hands, under the streetlights, until they arrived at the park.

'Just wait here,' Henry said to Lulu, when they got to the dimly lit barbecue gazebo. He plunged on into the park, which was shrouded in darkness. He scrambled up and over the pirate ship.

'Have you found her yet?' asked Lulu.

'Not yet,' he called back. He searched around the mini twister maypole and underneath the monkey bars.

He wished he were a sniffer dog. If he were a St Bernard, he could find that pony, even if it was buried metres and metres deep beneath the bark. He checked the seesaw and underneath the rope pyramid.

'What about now?'

'Still looking.' He wandered over to the nest swing and traced his steps away in circles, the bark sharp beneath his feet.

Holy Ramoley! No sign at all.

What if this big search had all been for nothing? He would not look so daring and brave then. He would just be silly and foolish. And if Mum or Dad found out, he would be in big trouble as well. They might ban him from eating bucketloads of gelato ever again. He needed to think. He needed to think good and hard and sensibly. He slumped down on the park bench. Something squirkled beneath his bottom. He leapt up, turned and patted the seat.

'Lulu!' he called. 'Lulu! I've found her.' And he scooped up the flattened, battered pony and ran across the park to Lulu, who was racing through the dark to him.

Henry lay back against his pillow. Dawn was coming. The night was cardigan grey and he could smell hot bread baking from across the road. A whole new day was nearly here. A whole new day!

Lulu was already sound asleep, breathing loudly, snoring even, like a baby dragon. He reached over and touched her face and felt Clover's plastic nose poking out beneath her chin. And it came to him suddenly, that in the dark of the night, he had found more than a battered, flattened pony. That in the worst moment of his fear, he had found the right sort of courage.

His skin sparked and his whole body sang.
Oh, gosh, he was ready. He was sure of it now. He was ready to face his silver bike. He was ready to learn to ride. He was ready to fly. He was ready.

A BRIGHT, LOUD LIFE

'So the thing is,' said Patch, pushing Henry's bike down the back street towards the inlet, 'if you want to learn quickly and you want to learn well, you're gonna have to trust me, okay? Because I know what needs to be done.'

Henry nodded. He felt a small flutter in his chest.

'Because we don't have long, yeah?' said Patch. 'Dad is only going to be at golf till just after lunch. But we can do it before then, you can do it, if you listen up and pay attention.'

'I will,' said Henry.

'Good man.' Patch cuffed Henry on the back of his head. 'Now, let's cross here.' They looked right and left and then darted across the road together.

Patch rolled the bike over the grass and then

onto the path. 'Now this is where we're gonna learn because there's not too many people around, yeah, and that's good. But also because there's a little hill here. It's just a tiny one, mind you, not a hill of death, so don't worry about that. But we need a tiny hill to help with the balance. Now, watch this.' And he flipped the bike over so it hung upside down, the wheels whizzing.

Patch swung his backpack down and unzipped it. He wrestled inside until he brought out a spanner.

Henry stooped over. 'What are you going to do with that thing?'

'I'm going to take off the pedals!' said Patch, crouching.

'Take off the pedals?' Henry wiped a sweaty palm against his short pocket. 'What! You can't do that! It's a new bike.' What would their dad say if they came back with no pedals? All the welcoming happiness would drain out of his eyes in a second!

'You've got to trust me!' said Patch. 'Remember?' He spun the spanner around and slipped a pedal off. He shoved it in the front pocket of his bag. He leapt up and darted around the front wheel.

Henry placed a hand on the back wheel to hold the bike steady. Patch twisted and turned the spanner once again. He whistled a tune as he dropped the second pedal into the bag. 'Now for the seat,' he said with a grin, flipping the bike back over.

'The seat!' Henry bit his lip. 'You're going to take the seat off?' How was he meant to ride a bike without a seat and without any pedals? He scraped his foot along the cement. He stopped and looked up. Holy Hamoley! Maybe Patch expected him to ride the bike like a circus monkey, doing handstands on the handlebars?

'I'm not a monkey, you know!'

'Ah, you big funny numpty,' said Patch. 'I'm not taking the seat off completely. I'm just lowering it. The thing is, you've got so used to riding a bike with training wheels that you can't balance for peanuts.' He shoved the seat down and tightened it. 'And that is the first thing we need to fix. So climb aboard.'

'Climb aboard? Now?'

'Dude!' said Patch. 'That's what we're here for, yeah?'

Henry closed his eyes. He was ready. He was almost sure of it. He wished he could summon up the electric spangles again, the singing through his whole body.

'Come on, mate!'

The sun was blaring and there was a sour taste in Henry's mouth. A tidal wave of sweat was rushing down his back. With any luck, it might sweep him off his feet and out to sea.

'Maybe I should wait one more year!'

'Nah,' said Patch, clapping his hand on Henry's shoulder. 'You don't want to do that. It's going to be dandy. But it's okay to be nervous, alright? I get nervous all the time.'

But Patch was so tall and strong and fast. Holy Moumoley! He was almost a man. He even had the faintest hint of a moustache, for goodness sake, sweeping across the top of his lip like a shadow. And he had real muscles, not like Henry, who had to prop his biceps up from below, and even then they were measly as walnuts.

'You don't believe me,' said Patch.

Henry shrugged. 'Well—'

'I get nervous about all sorts of stuff.'

'Like what?' Henry squinted up at Patch.

'Girls,' said Patch. 'Man, they make me nervous.'

It was like old times, how he and Patch used to chat at night, in their bunk beds, when they should have been asleep. Before Patch got a room of his own and started grunting and growling every time Henry took a step inside. Before his voice went all funny, dipping high and low, like a rollercoaster.

'There's this girl called Maeko at school…'

'Maeko?'

'Yeah…well, she's new to the school and we all call her "truth girl" because she is so whip-smart funny and clever and you know, whenever I see her, even when I just say hello, the palms of my hands get as itchy and sweaty as armpits, and next thing you know my tongue twists up and all my words spew

130

out higgledy-piggledy like someone dumped out a Scrabble bag in one go. I swear she thinks I'm the dumbest thing on two legs and she only says hi back because she feels sorry for me. On those miserable days, I kind of wish a boa constrictor would slither on by, swallow me whole and drag me down the fire stairs.'

'I heard about a man who got dressed up in a special snake-proof suit in the Amazon jungle and tried to feed himself to an anaconda,' said Henry.

Patch shuddered. 'Ah, dog-goggles,' he said. 'That's creepy.'

Henry rubbed his nose. 'He was filming the whole thing with cameras in his suit.'

'Whoah,' said Patch.

'It was like armour!'

'Yikes.'

'Because of the snake saliva and not wanting to get squished and all.'

Patch smooched his fringe back. 'What a fruitie!'

'I think he wore a rope around his foot so they could pull him out once he got...you know...all the way in!'

'Now that's a complete loony tune!'

'But I don't think there are any anacondas in Australia.' Henry glanced out at the inlet. The water was turquoise today. He turned and furtively checked the grass behind him. 'You know, there are one hundred and forty species of land snakes in Australia. That's a lot! It's kind of scary, when you start to think about it.'

'Okay, dude,' said Patch. 'Let's not think about land snakes. I feel we're getting off track here.'

Henry rubbed the back of his leg with his foot. 'We are?'

'The point of my story is not the boa constrictor.' Patch swiped a fist across his forehead.

'It's not?' asked Henry.

'Sheez, the point is…' Patch jabbed his foot into the pavement and sighed. 'Oh, gewsh, now I can barely remember what I was going to say. Hope I'm not turning into Dad. Next thing you know, I'll be losing my wallet and my keys every thirty seconds and blaming everybody else for it.'

'You were talking about a girl,' Henry said. 'Maeko.'

'Ah, yeah… brilliant… truth girl!' said Patch. 'Well, what I'm trying to say is that it's kind of normal to be nervous when you're doing something… new.'

'Okay,' said Henry.

'And even though I turn into a gibbering, nervous idiot every single time I run into Maeko, I'm going to keep on trying, because one day she'll recognise my scintillating intelligence, good looks and charm, my absolute and complete utter awesomeness, and want to go out with me forever.'

'Forever?'

'Okay, well, no, maybe not forever…aw, gosh, this little pep talk thingie…it's a tough gig. It's sort of not going as smoothly as I thought it would. I reckon being a footie coach might be harder than it looks. What I'm trying to say—' Patch scrunched up his face. 'What I'm trying to say…is that when you're nervous, it's good to keep the end in mind.'

Henry nodded. 'Okay,' he said. 'Keep the end in mind!'

'Excellento! So are you all set?'

Henry wiped the sweat out of his eyes. 'What end?'

'Holy Moley Pimento!' cried Patch. 'You, buddy, *you* – riding your bike down the bike path, on your own, no training wheels, speeding along like a little grand genius with the wind in your hair and the whole world watching. Okay?'

'Okay!'

'So let's get this show on the road—'

'But—'

'Figuratively,' said Patch. 'Sheezy-sweezy! When I say road, I mean path!'

'Alright then.' Henry swept his leg over the back of the bike and sat down on the seat. His sneakers rested solidly on the path.

'See, that's not so bad,' said Patch. 'Now, all I want you to do is to use your feet to push the bike along like you're running and then when you get enough speed, to lift your legs up, okay?'

'So I've got to just sort of run with my feet and make the bike go fast and then lift up my feet?'

'Exactly!'

Henry licked his lips. He pushed his feet forward. His front wheel wobbled like it had a life of its own, as if it was the boss of the joint.

'Hey, wait,' said Patch. He tugged on Henry's shirt. 'You've forgotten something.' He dug around in his backpack. 'Here! Your helmet.' He swung it over to Henry, who caught it with both hands.

Well! Holy Bamoley! That was almost fatal. The last thing Henry wanted was to have a fall and for his brain to end up like mashed potato. He slipped the helmet onto his head and snapped the lock together under his chin.

Patch placed his hand on Henry's head and tried to wobble the helmet. It was snug and tight. 'Perfect,' he said with a grin. 'Now go forth, mighty warrior, and conquer the lowlands!'

Henry nodded. He was a knight about to charge off into battle on his trusty steed. He swept his feet along the path.

'Hold the handlebars steady.' Patch jogged beside him. 'Yeah! Yeah! That's good. Keep going, mighty warrior.'

'I'm not sure,' said Henry.

'The holy grail is yours, sire!'

Holy Clamoley! His heart was thudding loudly. It was trampolining inside his chest, doing backflips even. The bike began to pick up speed. The front wheel rolled faster and faster. The wind whizzed in his ears.

'Yep,' said Patch, 'that's the ticket. Head up. Head up! Keep going. Keep pushing. And now lift your legs.'

Henry lifted his legs.

Out of the corner of his eye, the world reeled past. The solemn grey mountain. The flashes of turquoise from the inlet. The swing set, the Rotary garden and the gum trees. The fisherman by the edge of the water, the mangroves and the skate park. Every now and again, he struck a foot down like a long match against the path to increase his speed.

'I'm gliding,' Henry cried out, flicking his foot. The bike's front wheel wiggled uncontrollably. 'Yeeeeek!'

'Don't get too cocky,' said Patch, as he cantered alongside. 'Now pull up here and let's do it all again, until this balancing thing is as natural as breathing.'

For the next two hours, Henry rode up and down the small hill, over and over again, until he was drenched with sweat and could whip along the path on his bike without wobbling once.

After a morning tea of a pink finger bun, Henry

practised stopping and starting in the car park and Patch taught him how to turn both ways and do a figure eight. 'Well,' he said at last. 'I think you're ready.' And he yanked out his spanner and a pedal from the backpack.

'Are you going to put them back on now?' asked Henry.

'Only one to start with,' said Patch. 'So you get a bit of a taste of what it's like.'

So Henry practised shooting down the hill, with one foot on a pedal, the other scooting along the ground.

'We could leave it now, if you want,' said Patch. 'And come back tomorrow to do the rest?'

'Nope,' said Henry, his face dripping. 'I'm ready for two pedals!'

'You sure?'

'I'm sure!' Henry wanted to know now. He wanted more than a taste. He wanted to zoom across the world and to feel it rise up fast towards him at the same time.

'Alrighty, then,' said Patch. He spun the spanner up and caught it with one hand. 'Let's go.'

On Henry's first go with two pedals, he rampaged down the path, wobbling from side to side, before crashing through the Rotary garden. He toppled over a bushel of lavender and landed – splat – into another big scratchy bush.

'Geez,' said Patch, running up panting. He peered down. 'Are you okay?'

Henry felt the twinge. It was in his throat already. The howl. There was a scratch on his leg. Tiny beads of blood were beginning to bloom on his shin. He could give up and it would be okay. He had tried his best and there was always tomorrow.

'Far out,' said Patch. He took a step backwards and read the plaque at the front of the garden. 'Geez Louise! You've just crashed into a scent garden, Heno! Flat bang into a rosemary bush! No wonder it smells like roast leg of lamb in there!' He reached out his hand and pulled Henry up and dusted him down. 'That's a nasty scratch. Do you wanna take a break?'

Henry glanced over at the mountain at the back of the inlet. A fluff of cloud hung like a flung scarf. He gazed back at the dried-up scab in the middle of Patch's nose. He hesitated. He tried to grab hold of what Patch had said, how even confident, strong, almost-moustache big boys sometimes get jelly legs.

'It's fine,' said Patch. His face shone with sweat. 'You've done good! Better than could be expected. There's no shame in calling it a day! We can go back to camp and get a bandaid and come back again tomorrow, yeah?'

But there were not that many days left and Henry knew it. He wriggled his shoulders. He tipped his

head from side to side. He was pretty sure there
wasn't anything broken.

He ducked down and picked up his bike. A solid,
quiet certainty chinked in his chest. He was going to
keep the end in mind. That's what he was going to
do. He was going to ride his bike down the bike path.
He was going to sail on down, on his own, with no
training wheels, that afternoon.

After all, he wanted a bright, loud life.

The GRAND, GENIUS SUMMER

A squadron of seagulls squawked above Henry's head as he cycled down the bike path on his own. He was speeding along, his legs pumping hard. He felt the wind in his face, the sun on his skin and the shimmering cool breath of the water.

He wove his way around the sweaty joggers, the coconut girls, the greedy skateboarders and the big bikies on their rollerblades. He wobbled around the nuggety rugrats from next door, and the sunburnt power walkers with their frothing eager dogs. He pedalled harder and harder and snatched a glimpse of his shadow.

He belonged to the bike and the bike belonged to him.

He was sitting up high, like a king on a throne.

He was fast, cutting through space and time. He was light and free as a leaf carried a long way on a warm breeze.

He sailed past his dad, who was blowing bubbles for Lulu and Kale to pop.

He glided past his mum, who was sitting in a camp chair admiring the view.

He coasted past Reed, who was trudging home from the estuary empty-handed and grumpy.

He curved past Cassie, drifting along on her crimson dragster.

He pedalled all the way to the end of the park, where he made a sweeping turn on the grass, right outside the last ritzy-ditzy cabin, and then cycled all the way back, dinging his bell like it was Christmas and he was Santa bringing home the presents on his sleigh.

Everyone lined the path.

Patch, who was grinning wide as a clown and Mr Barone who was whistling loudly with his fingers and Mrs Barone who was snapping photos with her camera. Mr and Mrs Carson, who were whooping away, and open-mouthed Reed, and messy-haired Carey clutching a tattered *Calvin and Hobbes* collection, and sleepy-eyed Jay and Dylan who swung Kale quickly onto his shoulders, and Lulu who was hollering at Henry and clapping him in, like he was a soldier returning from war.

Dad stood just behind the crowd, still as a statue, the bubble wand slack in his hand. Henry cycled slowly over to him and stopped the bike right in front. A single bubble floated up between them.

Henry cleared his throat. His heart was ker-thudding like a drum. 'I'd really like to ride around to Nugget Rock,' he said, 'with you.' He gazed up at Dad, waiting for him to grin, waiting for him to laugh and whoo-hoo and clap his hands, waiting for his *exuberance*, the loudness of his rejoicing to come bubbling to the surface.

But Dad gazed back at him quietly. Then he pressed a hand hard to his chest, as if there was an ache in there that could barely be held. 'Aw, Heno,' he whispered, his eyes shiny. A crooked, wonky smile flitted across his mouth.

Henry wriggled his helmet and scratched his forehead. Had he done the right thing? Was his Dad happy or sad? Maybe he didn't want to cycle round to Nugget Rock now? Maybe the invitation had expired like a crusty coupon in the letterbox? Maybe some chances in life only came once?

'Aw, Hen-o,' said Dad again, his voice cracking.

Henry heard it then, in that tiny crack. It filled him with a strange and terrible wonder. There it was, love so big, so wild, brimming away in his dad's chest like a rising flood, close to bursting. 'Son of my heart,' whispered Dad. He dropped the bubble

141

wand and stepped forward and hugged Henry. And the hug was so big and bear-like and fierce, Henry's neck cricked and he laughed out loud, so glad to be wearing his bike helmet. But he felt his dad's delight. He felt it soak all the way through, like butter into hot bread.

And he wanted to tell Cassie. He did. He wanted to tell her she was right and that sometimes the very best things happen on the way to somewhere else. But when he turned to find her, she was gone.

'Here's to the grand, genius summer of Henry Hoobler!' cried Dad, lifting up Henry's arm exuberantly and waggling it about like floppy spaghetti.

'Whoo-hoooo!' yelled Patch, loping over. 'High five, you big numpty!'

Henry smacked his hand hard against Patch's palm. 'Thanks,' he said, gazing up.

'Ah, genius boy,' said Patch, flicking his fringe. 'I reckon you take after me in the scintillating intelligence, good looks and charm department, in my absolute and complete utter awesomeness.'

'There's no greater compliment!' said Dad, with a grin.

Henry's whole body tingled like he had jumped into a sea of bubbles.

'Yay!' said Lulu, galloping towards Henry across the grass. 'Yay! Neigh!'

'Oh, Henry Hoobler,' said Mum, running over to hug him. 'I'm so *proud* of you!'

And Henry grinned his head off as he accepted all the hugs and cheers and slaps of congratulations from everyone, even a feeble pat from smartypants Reed.

Oh, it was a grand, genius summer.

And Holy Zamoley, it sure tasted good!

STRAIGHT-UP
and TRUE

Henry wobbled to a stop. He leant his bike against a telegraph pole near Cassie's crimson dragster, down by the wharf. 'Hello there,' he said, unclicking his helmet.

'Hello, yourself!' said Cassie, peering up. She turned back quickly and swirled her bare feet in the water.

'I've been looking for you.'

A silver tinny buzzed past, out towards the breakwater. A lacy wake of water danced towards them. 'You disappeared so fast.' Henry sat down beside her. The water sloshed giddily against the edges of the stone wall. 'Where'd you go?'

'I had some stuff to do,' said Cassie, shrugging. 'The laundry and some shopping. And so...' She rubbed her knees. She lunged forward to fling a scrap of seaweed from her foot.

The water was green as glass.

Henry watched a large shadowy fish flit just above the reeds, a smaller school of fish drifting behind like a tiny speech bubble. He glanced over his shoulder. A lady in grey overalls and black gumboots was hosing down the deck of a fishing boat, tied up tight to the wharf. Everything ponged of fish.

Cassie sank her chin onto her hand. She stared hard into the water as if she was thinking about something extra tricky. She sat silently, her shoulders slumped, like someone had given her bad news.

Henry checked the palms of his hands secretly, just in case they were beginning to sweat. He rubbed them stealthily on the back of his shirt. Holy Macaroley, he hoped he wasn't about to suddenly turn into gibbering, nervous idiot like Patch! Maybe it was something a person could catch, like measles or chickenpox?

'Your bike...' said Cassie, in a small voice.

Henry froze. Dismay burst in the middle of his chest. It blazed out through his whole body like a fiery meteor shower. 'Oh,' he whispered.

'Before on the bike path,' said Cassie, 'when everyone was clapping and cheering...' She stopped.

Henry stared at his knees. It felt like the night roaring of the ocean was in his ears.

'It looked like...I don't know—'

Henry clenched his hands, till the tops of his knuckles shone.

'That you'd only just...learnt how to ride or something.'

Henry wiped his lips. 'Yes,' he murmured. His mouth was so dry.

'So. Then I got to...thinking about...your brakes.' Cassie cleared her throat. 'Were they ever—'

Henry shook his head. 'No.'

'Oh...' said Cassie, glancing over.

'They never were.' Misery oozed in Henry's stomach like a slick of oil.

Cassie turned and stared out towards the breakwater. 'So...it was just a big...lie?'

A swirl of fish scales glittered on the cement beside Henry's leg. He brushed them into a small pearly pile. 'I got the bike for Christmas. It's brand—'

'How come you didn't just say—'

'New.' Henry tugged at the neckband of his T-shirt. 'I don't know.' Something was panging away in his chest. 'I didn't want you to think I was—'

'I wouldn't have cared.'

'Some kind of baby,' finished Henry.

Two pelicans flew overhead, their wide wings whooping, their tummies sagging. Henry wondered how come they just didn't drop out of the sky.

He took a deep breath and gazed down at his shin, at the fresh graze from the morning.

'I like it when things are true.' Cassie snatched up a pebble and curled her fingers around it tightly. 'I don't like it when people pretend. When they say one thing and mean another. I don't like it how my mum says she is only going to sing one more time on a cruise ship and then she's going to come home forever. I don't like it how she tells me my dad loves me, when I've never even met him and he never even sends me a birthday card. I don't like it how she tells me we'll have a tin-roofed house by the sea one day, all of our own, when I know I'm going to live in a meerkat caravan always. I hate it how people make up stupid, dumb old stories to make themselves feel better, instead of telling things straight-up and true.'

A gust of wind blew across the water, wrinkling it like a skin. Cassie flung her arm back and tossed the pebble out as far as she could. It made a satisfying plop right near an old catamaran.

Henry watched the little circles ripple out bigger and bigger. Where would they go, those ripples? All the way to the other side of the world? Till they touched the toes of another girl, dangling her feet in the water from a stone wharf, filling her up with a longing for something big and true?

Oh, blimey, he had let that dumb old story about his bike brakes slip out, almost by accident. But then he let it stay out. He pretended he could ride, even when he couldn't. He didn't realise how telling a tiny, stupid story to make himself feel better could possibly make someone feel worse. But now he knew. He could see it. Cassie cut off and adrift, sucked away by a fast current, more left out and lonely than before.

Oh, gosh, there was something weighty, sharp-cornered and icy-cold fierce smarting right in the middle of his chest. There was a word in his mouth, hot as a star.

'Sorry,' he whispered.

Cassie glanced at him. Their eyes met and held.

'I'm sorry I wasn't . . . straight-up and true.'

Cassie's mouth quivered and she turned away quickly towards the wharf, as if something very fascinating was happening there, like the world's biggest fish had just been caught.

Henry ducked his head. He watched the breeze sweep this way and that way, until it winked out, just like that. A bunch of little kids squealed on the big nest swing across the water. His throat ached and he suddenly felt so tired, like he hadn't slept in a hundred years.

'It's okay, you know,' Cassie murmured. She brushed a hand across her cheek. 'I mean . . . it's just . . . I understand . . . and it's a very big bike.' She glanced over her shoulder and stared at it, glinting silver in the sun. 'Probably, if you think

148

about it…everyone in the whole world would be worried about riding that thing for the very first time.'

Henry felt a sharp twinge of relief. 'Everyone in the whole world?' he breathed.

'Yes,' said Cassie.

'Even Donald Bradman?' He could feel a kind of gladness humming right through him.

'Especially the Don!' said Cassie. 'Imagine if he'd fallen off a bike like that and broken his arm. He might never have ever played for Australia!'

'Ha!' said Henry.

'The whole history of cricket would never be the same!' said Cassie. 'So there!'

Henry bent the toe of his sneaker back. 'That would have been one terrible Worst Case Scenario,' he said, with a lopsided grin.

'I know,' said Cassie, smiling.

They watched a long line of cyclists, small as ants, meander up the hill to the lookout.

Cassie nodded. 'Have you been for a ride out there yet?'

'I just came back.'

'Where'd you go?'

'All the way to the lookout and then down to Nugget Rock.'

'Did you see any seals?'

'Nope! Not a single one.'

149

Cassie dipped her fingers into the water. She splashed her face gently. 'Did you like it?' she asked, rubbing the bottom of her T-shirt across her cheeks.

'I raced my dad,' said Henry, 'down the tiniest hill and he gave the biggest, scariest screech I've ever heard, because I think he was worried about what my mum would do to him if I fell off and got *maimed.*'

'Maimed,' said Cassie. 'Your dad. He's so—'

Henry nodded. 'I know.'

'Funny.' Cassie sighed. She stretched her T-shirt out.

A seagull bobbed on the water, floating up close to their feet, like it was eavesdropping. Henry itched his nose against his shoulder. It was true. His dad *was* funny. It was like he was always expecting some good thing to happen, just around the corner.

'You know, when Patch was little he thought all seagulls were called sea girls!' said Henry. 'And every time we eat fish and chips now, Dad always says, *Hey, Patch, here come all your sea girls!*'

'Sea girls,' said Cassie, laughing.

Henry wanted to ask Cassie a question. It was roosting in his head like a bird. But he wasn't sure. Maybe some questions weren't right to ask, especially if they were snoopy and nosy and made someone's heart sorer than before. But then again, what if he didn't ask? What if no one asked anything important, just slunk back into their shells like shy snails? Would that leave people sometimes feeling lonelier than ever before?

'Is it true?' he asked slowly. 'About your dad...that you've never ever...and the...birthday card and everything?'

Cassie rested her chin on her knee. 'Well, you know, my dad...he left before I was born. He's a musician. He used to play banjo in the city, beneath the statue of Queen Victoria. That's where my mum met him. She said it was love at first sight and he had a voice like an angel. I'd like to hear him sing. I would. But my Pop reckons he's a no-hoper.'

'A what?' asked Henry.

'A no-hoper.'

'What does that mean?'

'I'm not sure.'

Henry wrinkled his nose. 'Is it a person without any hopes?'

'Maybe,' said Cassie. 'But I think my Pop meant it in a different way. Like my dad is a not a person to hope in.'

The sun baked down and seared so loud, Henry's eyes hurt. He thought about his exuberant, buoyant, happy Dad and his big, wild, brimming love and how good a butter-into-hot-bread hug felt and how strange and unthinkable it seemed that a person couldn't hope in their own dad.

'Where is he now?' asked Henry.

'No one knows.' Cassie flicked a small stone into the water. 'Maybe he's singing in Rome, in front of a fountain, with all the pigeons pecking about his feet. Or maybe he's singing love songs on a bridge in Paris, for all the couples about to propose. Or maybe he's not singing at all anymore. Maybe's he's given up on all that and he's married to someone new and he goes to work every day and does a yucky, boring job and the best part is when he comes home, all tired out from working with numbers, to a little girl and a little boy who run to the front door when they hear the garden gate open with a big squeak.'

Henry shook his head. 'Oh, wow!'

'I don't mind,' said Cassie, shrugging. 'Because my Pop is very good to me, you know. Even if he's a bit grumpy now. My Nan used to say my Pop likes to pretend he's a peanut brittle chocolate, so no one will ever know he's really a big old strawberry cream.'

A family rode by on their bikes, shouting and laughing and ringing their bells, racing each other down the path.

'Do you reckon—' Henry stopped.

'What?'

'I'm wondering,' said Henry, glancing at the family, 'if you'd want to—'

'Go for a ride?' Cassie scrambled to kneel up. 'YES. Oh, yes. I would!'

'Excellento,' said Henry. 'But where shall we go?'

Cassie clutched suddenly at Henry's elbow. 'Look! Out there! It's Heathcliff.'

'What?' asked Henry. 'Where?'

'See the ripple,' said Cassie. 'Near the wharf!'

Henry made binoculars out of his hands.

'He's gone for a cruise around the edge of the dock but he'll be here in a minute,' said Cassie. She pulled out a little plastic bag from the pocket of her backpack. 'The charter boats came back early because it was so rough out at the island. Everyone was gutting fish and there were so many birds and so many stingrays, so much snatching and grabbing. You know, sometimes the birds steal a scrap right out of another bird's beak and poo in the water with happiness at exactly the same time.'

'Holy Wamoley!' said Henry, dropping his hands.

'I know,' said Cassie. 'It's so gross. Just wham bam squirt – big white cloud.'

'Oh, geez!' said Henry.

'Now take Heathcliff. He has very good manners. Mostly he prefers a pat to a feed. So sometimes he misses out on eating. So I like to hang around to give him a little bit extra. Here he comes!'

'Holy Guacamole!' cried Henry, as the stingray swam towards them. He shuffled backwards. 'He's almost as big as a coffee table.'

Cassie grinned. 'My Pop reckons he's like a gigantic fishy pool cleaner.'

'He's much bigger than I expected,' said Henry, shivering. He tucked his legs up tight.

'I know,' said Cassie, opening up the plastic bag and scooping out another sliver of squid. She dropped it into the water. 'But remember, he's not dangerous and he's very friendly.'

The sun went behind a long tuft of cloud.

'He looks a lot like the Millennium Falcon.'

'The what?'

'You know, like Han Solo's ship in *Star Wars*.'

'Oh, yeah,' said Cassie. She dropped another scrap of squid in and then ducked down and rolled over onto her stomach. Her eyes followed Heathcliff as he swooped past.

'It must be hard,' said Henry. 'Without his whole tail.'

'I know. It's not good. He doesn't have any protection now because he doesn't have a barb. Sometimes I worry about that at night.' Cassie splashed her hands in the water. Heathcliff drifted back towards them and she bent right down and stroked her hand along his skin. 'Do you want me to tell you something?' Henry could see a tiny scar on her cheek, like a small crescent moon.

'Sure,' he said.

'I tell Heathcliff *everything*!'

A small spark of sadness flared in Henry. 'What sort of things?'

Heathcliff nudged Cassie's hand. She laughed and reached out again to pat him. 'Oh, well... all sorts of stuff. Sometimes I talk to him about my Pop and the arthritis in his fingers that aches so bad in the winter that his fingers curl over and how it makes him crankier than a cut snake. And sometimes I talk to Heathcliff about my mum and the things I remember from when I was little. Like the marshmallow smell of her hair and the sound of her singing me to sleep. And sometimes I make wishes.'

'What sort of wishes?'

'Sometimes I wish for my mum's cruise ship to stay afloat and not get hit by bad storms. And sometimes I wish my Nan would send a big shooting star, so I know she's still thinking of me, even in heaven. And sometimes I wish my Pop would tell jokes like he used to, even the bad old ones he's told a million times before and sometimes I wish people never went away. I wish that the most. I wish people stayed forever and there was no more missing anywhere. No more pinching just here.' She pressed a hand against her chest.

Henry nodded. He watched Heathcliff swirl towards them again. 'You know what I wish?' he said.

'No.'

Heathcliff whirled past and Henry gazed at his missing tail. 'I wish every sad thing would come untrue.'

'Ah, yes,' said Cassie. 'Me too! I wish that too.'

155

Heathcliff wheeled by again like a superhero with a rippling black cape.

'You can pat him,' said Cassie softly. 'If you want.'

Henry swallowed. He could. He could reach out with his hand and touch Heathcliff, just one tiny little stroke with the tips of his fingers. But then again, Heathcliff wasn't a cat or a dog or a guinea pig or a budgie. He wasn't tame like that. He was still a wild creature, even without most of his tail.

There was a fluttering feeling in Henry's chest, a tiny buzzing frenzy. He inched closer to the edge. It was normal to be nervous. He had to remember that. He hunched over and gazed into the water.

'Heathcliff's making a circuit,' said Cassie. 'He'll come round again in a sec. Get ready!' She dug into her plastic bag and dropped in another piece of squid. 'Won't be long now!'

Henry rubbed the palms of his hands against his shorts. The bravest people were the ones who were scared and did brave things anyway. They were more brave than the people who did daring things without a second thought. It looped in Henry's head like a catchy chorus from a song.

'It's okay,' said Cassie. She was grinning at him. Her eyes were trophy gold and gleaming. And he knew it didn't matter that his legs were shaky and his tummy was gurgling loudly. It didn't matter if he got it right or wrong.

'Here he comes!' Heathcliff flew like a bird above the reeds, rising higher and higher, swift as a shadow.

Henry wriggled forward on his knees and then lunged out, dipping his hand into the water. With one long flap of his wings, Heathcliff swooped by, his blunt snout breaking the surface. And Henry stretched out and stroked his speckled back, the skin sandpapery as a kitten's tongue. 'Holy Raymoley!' he whispered.

Heathcliff rolled and spun and flapped. He ducked and dived and circled back, rising up, alive and playful, funny as a puppy and yet the fiercest and wildest animal Henry had ever touched.

The sun burst out. The whole sea blazed with spangles of light. Henry gazed down, bedazzled and silent, his fingertips tingling.

'I did it,' he breathed.

'You did!' cried Cassie.

Heathcliff turned and coasted away with one creamy flutter of his wings, out towards the catamaran.

'Hey!' called Henry. 'Come back!'

'He will,' said Cassie. 'Don't worry. He likes you. He's not playful like that with everyone.'

Henry clutched his dripping hand to his chest. It came to him that he hadn't fallen off the stone ledge and landed on top of Heathcliff and been carried out into the deep and slipped off and ended up being swallowed by a whale shark! It dawned on him that his Worst Case Scenario had not happened at all. He started to chuckle.

'What?' asked Cassie, smiling.

'I don't know,' said Henry. It was impossible for him to put it into words. How he could sense some kind of fierce, trembling wildness rise up in him too. Some determination not to let the worry about the terrible things that *might* happen stop him from enjoying the grand, genius good things right before him.

'Here he comes again!' said Cassie.

Henry dunked both hands in the water. When Heathcliff swirled past and rose up, he and Cassie patted him together.

Then Henry closed his eyes and made some big wishes about calm seas and shooting stars and bad old jokes, hoping Heathcliff might carry them out to sea, through the shallow patches of turquoise and teal, through the shimmering splashes of kingfisher blue, through the pools of sapphire and indigo, right out into the listening deep.

MAGiC

Henry and Cassie whizzed along the bike path, side by side, past the fishing boats, their front wheels spinning in time. 'Your bike is very flash,' called Cassie, grinning.

'Whoah-hoah!' Henry was concentrating super hard to keep it in a straight line. He didn't want to suddenly wobble and plough into Cassie and make them both fall off in a tangled heap.

'It's a super streaky, flashety-flash lightning bolt.'

'Yeah.'

'Does it have a name?'

Henry jerked the handlebars to straighten them up. 'Nope.'

'You should give it one.'

'I should?'

'For sure!'

'Like what?'

'I don't know. Maybe Thunder,' said Cassie. She stood up and pedalled harder past the Olympic pool. 'Or Tinkerbell or Uncle Steve or the Breezer or the Flying Banana or Merlin or Hi-Ho Silver Away?'

'Is that right?' Henry pedalled furiously to catch up.

Cassie glanced at Henry as they coasted along. 'My Nan always used to say that everything works better with a name. Fridges. Washing machines. Cars. Bikes. Teapots.'

'Does your bike have a name?'

Cassie swerved around a chalk-drawn mermaid on the path. 'Sure thing! My bike is called Blinter. It's a Scottish word for the special way stars dazzle on a winter's night. My Nan helped me choose it.'

'What if I named my bike after some stars or something?' asked Henry.

'Whoah-yeah!' Cassie veered across the path and onto the grass for a second. 'Yeeee-ess!' she puffed, darting back. 'A constellation! I like it! You could call it Pegasus the flying horse or Hercules or Lynx – or Orion the Hunter! He is massive and has a belt of three stars that you can see in the sky! What do you reckon?'

'Hmmmm.' Henry dodged around a toddler riding a skateboard down the path on his tummy.

'What about Sirius? That's the brightest star in the sky and Chinese people call it the Celestial Wolf!'

Celestial Wolf! Henry's front wheel wobbled. Holy Chamoley! That was a little bit too close to werewolves for his liking.

All the names Cassie was suggesting were grander and more genius than he could ever live up to! But then again, maybe it was a good idea to have something a little out of the ordinary, sort of as an encouragement? One of his friends from school was called Tom Desmond Tutu Wilson because Tom's parents believed in aspirational middle names as well as plain, ordinary first ones.

When Henry first heard Tom's middle name, he had to go home and ask his Mum what an aspirational name meant. She said she guessed Tom's parents wanted him to have a middle name that gave him something juicy to aim for with his life because Desmond Tutu was famous for being an extraordinary man of peace and laughter. Which seemed kind of funny to Henry given that Tom Desmond Tutu Wilson did not even really like to smile, ever.

'You know a lot about stars!' said Henry.

'I know!'

They each overtook a pack of nuggety rugrats in spiky bike helmets, even though their small legs were spinning in fast-forward. Henry felt a tiny spurt of triumph as he sailed past them.

Cassie slid back across the grass to his side. 'Well, that's because of my mum! She has a different name when she sings on stage because she thinks her real name is too boring for someone who wants to be a famous singer. When she sings on stage, everyone calls her Ursa Major. She named herself after a bear constellation that you can see pretty much everywhere in the world. That's how she signs her autographs too, for all her fans on the cruise ships, even though her real name is Deirdre Evans.'

'Ursa Major,' said Henry, tasting the words.

'Uh-huh! It's very dramatic! That's what my Nan always said.' Cassie clicked her tongue. 'But very crazy things are always happening to my mum, so it probably suits her.' They cycled down past the cabins under the pines, their front verandahs brimming with bikes.

Henry pondered the names. He liked the idea of Orion. It sounded strong and brilliant. But he wasn't really a hunter, not at heart, not in the true sense. He wasn't sure that seeking out small funny moments counted, even though that was treasure to him and made the whole world shine. He darted around an abandoned trike. It would be a grand, genius thing to have a winged horse, though. And wasn't that the very thing Patch said he loved about riding, how it was like flying? If he called his bike Pegasus, he would

162

always remember Patch teaching him how to ride and summer and the smell of rosemary and trying hard to keep on going, even when he most wanted to give up.

'Pegasus,' said Henry. 'That's it! Maybe Peg for short.'

Cassie rang her bell. It chimed out loud and clear. 'Welcome, oh, mighty Peg, to the bike paths of Yelonga. May they bring you magic, oh magnificent one.'

Henry laughed. Magnificent one! He couldn't help thinking Cassie had caught a little bit of her mum's crazy.

'Now come on!' she called, tossing her head. 'Let's race because I want to show you everything there is to see!'

Cassie took Henry to all her favourite spots.

While they were cycling along the boardwalk, they saw a snow-white eagle hover on a breeze above the inlet. They watched the Yelonga Bridge rise up slowly for a single sailboat. They slurped a strawberry milkshake at the Old Palace Café and hand-fed a school of fish off the front jetty.

'Let's go to one more place,' said Cassie. 'Please! They'll be there now. I know you'll like it.'

And Cassie took Henry back out to Nugget Rock, where he had been earlier with his dad. They slipped and slithered over sandstone blocks, on shaky tired legs, creeping down close to the water.

'Holy Flubbamoley!' breathed Henry.

Five big seals were soaking up the sun on the rocks, lazing about like fat brown slugs.

Cassie nodded. 'Amazing, huh?'

'I've never seen anything like this! Well, only at the zoo.'

'I know,' said Cassie, her eyes sparkling. 'When I first saw them, I thought they were fake. But these ones come from the colony that live out at Lorelle Island, where the lighthouse is. My Nan reckoned these are the party-pooper seals, who would prefer a good book in an armchair to a night dancing up a storm.'

Henry hunched down, waiting for one of these seals to move. 'Do they have names?' he asked.

'Now you're getting it.' Cassie nudged him with her elbow. 'When my Nan was little, she lived on a farm and so she named all those seals after her favourite cows because she thought their eyes were so similar, all warm and chocolatey. And all they do is sleep and eat. So the one with the bird poo on her back is Bluebell. And the one with the chunk out of her tail is Hazel.' She nodded. 'And that one over there, lying on her back, is Buttercup and the one getting splashed by the water is Daisy. And that huge one over there with the reddish coat is Myrtle, who is always grumpy, especially if she gets woken up.'

'Their noses are so pointy,' said Henry.

Cassie lifted her eyebrows. 'Uh-huh!'

'They look like dogs without legs, don't you reckon?' said Henry.

'I never thought of that,' said Cassie.

'Log dogs,' said Henry.

Cassie laughed. 'Log dogs! I like that!'

Henry felt a thrill. He liked the way Cassie's laugh burst out, so loud and free, like a person busting out of a birthday cake. Myrtle rolled over and opened one cranky eye.

'Do they ever dive in and swim?' Henry whispered.

'I don't think they're going to move today,' murmured Cassie. 'I'm telling you, they're just too stubbornly comfortable!'

'Oh, bummer,' breathed Henry, glancing sideways. 'That's a shame.'

Cassie jumped up. 'But we can still ride to the end of the breakwater.'

So Cassie and Henry clambered back over the rocks and snatched up their bikes and rode down the sandy path, right to the end of the breakwater. They perched on the point and gazed for ages at the motorboats zooming out across the bar as if they were in an action movie, foam spraying behind them.

Then just before it was time to go, Henry stroked

the fool's gold of Nugget Rock like a lucky charm
and only a few seconds later, he saw Myrtle roll off
and speed by in the water, swift as a rocket. It hardly
seemed possible that only a moment before, she
was lolling about as if sleep was the only thing on
her mind.

'Look,' said Cassie. She dragged Henry up onto
her rock and pointed to the entrance. A school of
dolphins rose up in a wave, their grey bodies sleek
and glistening.

'Holy Dolphamoley!' whispered Henry.

It was magic.

Patting Heathcliff. Riding Peg. Spotting the snow-
white eagle. Waiting for the rising bridge. Feeding
the fish. Seeing Myrtle swim. Watching the dolphins
surf. Exploring a whole world he didn't even know
was out there. But as Henry and Cassie rode back
through clouds of sea salt, he knew the best magic of
all was finding a straight-up and true friend. He knew
there was nothing more magic than that!

At HOME
in the WORLD

Henry checked the tables again. They were decked out for the party, with plastic red-checked tablecloths, shells from the beach and small white candles. He counted the chairs. 'Are you sure you've got enough? For everybody?' His tummy was churning. He wanted everything to be perfect.

'I am,' said Mum. 'Enough for everyone. All of us. Hooblers. Carsons and Barones. I also borrowed two extra chairs from the recreation room for Cassie and her grandfather.'

'Second-last night,' said Dad. He chumped Henry in the arm. 'It'll be back to school before you know it. Year Three. You'll be up with the big kids. How do you feel about that?'

Henry shrugged his dad's hand away. He didn't

want to think about the second-last night. He didn't
want to think about going back to school or moving
up to Year Three. He didn't want to think about
big kids with their grazed knees and fierce eyes and
handball playing. He didn't want to think about
saying goodbye to Yelonga. He didn't want to think
about saying goodbye to Cassie.

He counted the cups and the serviettes again.
'Are you sure they're coming?'

'Her grandfather said they would,' said Mum.

'Did you tell him it was a *hat* party?'

'I did,' said Mum. She was wearing a lime green
witch's hat with foamy black netting, sprinkled with
spiders and bugs.

'What did he say?'

'Well, he said he thought he could hunt
something up and that it wouldn't be a problem.'

'Did he seem grumpy?'

'No. I don't think so,' said Mum.

'What about the tarp?' asked Henry, gazing at his
dad. 'Have you tightened it?'

'Well, no,' said Dad.

'But her Pop hates loose tarps!'

'I think the tarp will be okay for tonight, mate,'
said Dad, scooping up some platters of green salad.
'Not too flappy. There's not a lot of wind.'

'And he's not very fond of tourists!' said Henry.
'That's what Cassie said!'

'Now, Henry,' said Mum, gently, 'we can only be who we are.'

'I think everything will be okay,' said Dad. 'After all, Cassie's been over here for lunch and dinner nearly every day and you two have been riding around the countryside, swimming in the pool, jumping on the giant pillow—'

'Snorkelling in the Hole!' interrupted Mum.

'Whacking each other senseless at totem tennis,' said Patch, bringing out the drinks. He was wearing a Viking helmet, which kept slipping down his forehead.

'And chasing little blue crabs!' added Lulu, galloping about in a giant brown glossy papier-mache horse head.

'If her Pop wasn't keen on that, I'm sure he would have said something. You need to settle, son of my heart!'

'Her Pop seemed like a perfectly ordinary man to me,' said Mum. 'Only a little more sunburnt than average.'

Henry groaned. 'But what if he doesn't like curry? Why couldn't we do a pasta night?'

'There's plenty of salads and bread rolls,' said Dad, plopping down the platters on the main tables.

'Cassie said he likes to eat plain food.'

Mum neatened up the platters, moving them away from the candles. 'I'm sure he will be fine.'

'Some people don't like spicy, hot food because it gives them ... well, you know what—'

'Runny bot-bot!' said Dad.

'Daniel!' Mum whirled around.

Dad grinned. 'Not to mention a burning ring of fire.'

'Oh, Daddy!' said Lulu. 'That's rude!'

'Sorry!' Dad pressed a hand against his mouth. He flicked a pink plait over his shoulder.

'Maybe Dad shouldn't wear that wig,' said Henry. 'And I don't think a tiara counts as a hat!'

'Don't worry,' said Dad. 'I've got a police cap to wear over the top of it.'

'But what if he thinks Dad's a bit, you know ... bonkers?' asked Henry.

Mum's lips twitched. 'Ah, well, Henry ...'

Henry touched his bike helmet. His dad had strung a forest of cable ties through it to make it look more crazy and exciting, as if at any moment a flock of magpies would swoop down and pluck his eyes out.

'Do you think I look like an echidna?' Henry flicked the cable ties sticking up like spikes. He followed his mum around the table, as she straightened up the place settings.

'Not at all,' said Mum, glancing over. 'But if you'd like a different hat, I've still got a spare sombrero.'

'No,' said Henry. He had tried on some other hats in the tent earlier that afternoon, a leprechaun hat

170

and a propeller cap, but neither of them felt right. It was like an insult to even try another hat on, especially when his bike helmet had given him the most fun in the past few days. Holy Tramoley! The truth was maybe no other hat made him quite as comfy.

'Ha-ha, Henry,' said Dad. 'There's no need to worry. Here comes Cassie and her Pop now.'

They came waltzing through the twilight, under the pines and across the grass, Cassie skipping ahead, her Pop bow-legged and gallant, as if he was summoning up pluck and courage.

'What is that thingie on his head?' Lulu stopped mid-gallop.

'I believe that would be a traffic cone,' said Dad.

'A different kind of witch's hat altogether,' said Mum, with a laugh.

'Oh, wow, so cool,' said Patch, the horn of his Viking helmet snagging on a tent line. 'It's got a flashing light inside it.'

Dad stamped a foot. 'Now, that *is* the spirit,' he exclaimed.

'And look!' Lulu pointed. 'Cassie's got a nest for a hat!'

'A *magpie* nest,' said Dad, arching his eyebrows at Henry.

'Sheez,' said Patch. He flicked the cable ties on Henry's helmet. 'You'd better watch out, sunshine!'

'Welcome,' said Mum, walking towards Cassie and

171

Pop, her arms outstretched. 'Can I get you both a drink?'

'You're so tall!' cried Lulu. She looked up at Cassie's grandfather, her mouth wide open. 'Like a lighthouse!'

'And this must be Lulu!' said Pop, bending down to shake her hand. 'How do you do?'

'I'm good.' Lulu tilted her head. 'Would you like to meet my ponies?'

'Of course,' said Pop.

'All of them?'

Pop bowed his head. 'Every single one!'

'None of them are my favourite,' she confided, leading Pop to a camp chair. 'I love them all. Every single one!'

'I'm glad to hear that!' said Pop.

'Oh, Lulu!' said Mum. 'Let poor Frank have a drink and a chat first before you stampede him with ponies.'

'No, no, no,' said Pop. 'I would love to meet them now. It would be a great privilege and a pleasure.'

Dad turned and winked at Henry. 'See, matie! Nothing to worry about!'

The tightness in Henry's chest eased. He smiled tentatively and gazed up. The whole sky was iced with cloud, long dusky ribbons of light, glimmering like party streamers.

Everyone sat at the long table together, their funny hats bobbing up and down as they laughed and chatted. They lifted their faded plastic cups and chinked them together, calling out 'Cheers!' and 'Here's to our second-last night' and 'Hurrah for holidays.' Then they passed around platters and piled up their plates with rice, chicken tikka masala, butternut pumpkin curry, gobi aloo, beef biryani and butter chicken.

The moon shone like a paper lantern.

People strolled by on the bike path: the big bikie with the steel-wool beard and his bikie mates, the nuggety rugrats from next door and the coconut girls. They all stopped to stare, taken aback and then delighted to see a long table of people wearing funny hats.

Dad lifted a glass in their direction and offered a toast. The big bikie with the steel-wool beard laughed and clapped. 'I want a helmet like that one,' he cried, pointing at Henry.

The coconut girls and the nuggety rugrats from next door danced and weaved their way down the path into the dusk, ringing bike bells, giggling and shouting with excitement, as if they were taking a piece of the party with them.

Henry wiped his soft naan bread across his plate, swooshing up the last bit of butter chicken sauce. It was good. So good! He could tell Cassie's Pop was having a good time too. He was stretching back in his chair and patting his tummy, as if he couldn't fit another thing in. And then Lulu tugged on his arm and asked him to tell them a story. He nodded his head and rested a large veiny hand on top of her little one.

'So it's a big story you're wanting?' asked Pop, nodding gravely.

'Yes,' said Lulu. 'With adventure and shipwrecks and great white sharks and pirates and maybe even a pony.'

'I'm not sure about a pony!' said Pop, with a hearty laugh.

'How about a Princess?' asked Lulu.

Pop winked. 'How about an orangutan?'

'Yes!' breathed Lulu, clutching her hands tight.

And Pop told them about the time when he was a younger man and sailed his way around the world in a wooden boat he had built himself, navigating by the stars and travelling by wind. He told them about how a pod of whales once sang him to safety on the inkiest of nights and how he once saw orangutans, orange as the setting sun, swinging from some trees in Borneo.

'Really?' asked Lulu.

'I swear,' said Pop. 'I barely breathed because I was scared the slightest sigh might scare them off.'

'What did you eat?' asked Dylan. The bells on his jester hat jingled. 'You know, while you were on the boat?'

'Mostly fresh fish and the hard vegies like carrots and potatoes. Some barley, rice, oats and pre-sprouted beans. And lots of tinned food. Baked beans. Tuna. Creamed rice pudding was a treat,' said Pop. He adjusted the traffic cone on his head. 'But one time, on an island, some friendly villagers gave me fifty-eight green bananas and I strung them up around the boat, in every nook and cranny, and ate one a day until they were gone.'

'And you saw lots of animals,' said Lulu. 'But no ponies.'

'No ponies, I'm very sorry to say,' said Pop, shaking his head. 'But I did see pink iguanas and swam with the seals on the Galapagos Islands and chatted to a lot of fish, stingrays and turtles along the way too.'

'Pink iguanas!' said Lulu. 'That's almost as good as pink ponies!'

'Almost,' said Pop, chuckling. 'I like that!'

Reed leant forward. The corks on his slouch hat swung about his face. 'But what about great white sharks?'

'Aaaah, yes!' Pop stretched back and crossed his arms. Candlelight flickered across his face. 'There was this one time, when there were a lot of different schools of fish about. I had a line in the water, when – bang – with one gigantic tug, my whole rod flew overboard. I peered over and a giant great white shark surged up, teeth bared. It rolled over on its side and gave me the eyeball. I hoisted the sail and got out of there quick-sticks, but wouldn't you know it, the darned thing swam alongside, like a ghost. Then just when I thought I had given it the shake, it leapt out of the water like a holy whale and had an almighty chew on the back of the boat, before sliding off and swimming away. I swear to God, I was so shaky I nearly fell overboard.'

Reed shivered. 'It was lucky you didn't die of a heart attack.'

'You're telling me,' said Pop, with a grin.

Jay snatched up a piece of naan bread. 'Did you see anything else?'

'How about a live volcano shooting out sparks all through the night?'

Carey slid off his Dr Seuss hat. He crumpled it in his hands. 'No way!'

'Cross my heart,' grinned Pop.

'What about the hard bits?' asked Mr Barone, his Tutankhamun hat glinting gold. He plopped a slice of coconut banana into his mouth.

Pop sighed. 'Well, there's always something breaking on a boat and so much fixing and hoping against hope to make it to the next port before everything goes bung again.' He shuffled forwards in his chair and pinched his lip. 'And then there are the doldrums, when the wind leaves a sailor altogether.

One time I was motionless in the ocean for a month until I thought I might go crazy. And there are pirates and sea gypsies disguised as fishermen, and hundred-foot waves.'

'Hundred-foot waves!' gasped Reed.

'But then there are nights,' said Pop, 'when veils of light trail beneath the boat, like the sea has swallowed the whole sky and I'm sailing a galaxy, and it makes a man glad to be alive. It does.'

Mum fell back against her chair. 'Oh, my, that sounds so amazing!'

'Yes!' breathed Reed. 'I want to hear more.'

Pop's face was soft with remembering. 'Ah, you're too kind,' he said, rubbing his knees and smiling sheepishly. 'Listening to an old man rabbit on and on.'

'Not at all,' said Dad. 'It's a privilege. Gosh. Wow! There's so much juicy goodness in the world.'

Pop scratched his nose and scooched forward. 'Ah, yes... but sometimes, you know, the world, it goes off-kilter no matter where you are and everything can appear as strange as a new country. Things haven't been the same for me since my wife Nance died. Ah, golly, she was the only princess for me.' He nodded at Lulu and gave a watery smile. 'North star. Ballast. She was the whole anchor of my life.'

'Oh, yes,' said Mum. 'Of course.'

Pop cleared his throat. 'But I want to thank you

all for welcoming Cassie. She's had a tough time this past year, but I know she's enjoyed every second with you. Maybe it's a true thing that it takes people from away to make a local feel at home in the world again.'

'Ah, Frank,' said Mum. She stretched over Lulu to press a hand gently against his shoulder. 'It's been a pleasure to have Cassie around.'

Dad nodded. 'A delight from start to finish. And it's been great to get to know you too, Frank. You've given me a grand, genius idea for a future holiday, that's for sure.'

Mrs Barone snorted. 'Does it involve a sailing boat and an ocean?'

'Perhaps,' said Dad, lifting an eyebrow.

Henry felt a little flutter in his chest.

Holy Swamoley! Did his dad just not hear that whole story about the great white shark and the hundred-foot waves and the pirates and sea gypsies?

Although Henry had to admit it would be pretty grand to sail veils of light in the ocean. He knew this was called *bioluminescence* because Andrew Chichester, the genius in his class, had spoken about it for news. He had treasured up that word because it was the longest one he'd ever heard.

'Well, folks, is there something I can do for you… anything…to show my gratitude, before you head home?'

'Ah, no,' said Dad. 'Geez, Frank. Please.'

But something zapped inside Henry, like a bug

against a blue light. He sat up straight. 'Well, there is one thing!'

'Henry,' said Mum, opening her eyes wide.

Pop beamed. 'You name it.'

Henry gazed down the table. He hesitated. 'Well... you know... I'm thinking...' He took a deep breath. 'That Reed... would love to catch a... kingie.'

'A kingie?' asked Pop. 'Is that right?'

'Yes,' said Lulu. 'Because Reed hasn't caught a thing, the WHOLE holidays. Not one single fish. Not even a gumboot. Even though he's gone out fishing nearly *every single day.*'

'Oh, Lulu,' said Henry. 'Shhhhhh!' Because this was the thing he was pondering; maybe a grand, genius holiday wasn't a grand, genius holiday if someone nearby was feeling horribly miserable, even if that person happened to be an infuriating bossy-boots smartypants!

Reed stared back at Henry. His lips were moving up and down, as if he wanted to speak but all the words were popping like bubbles before they made it out of his mouth.

'Consider it done.' Pop winked at Reed. 'You and your dad meet me at the wharf at five sharp tomorrow morning and I'll take you out to the reef. I know the secret haunts of the kingfish and it would be a pleasure to help you.'

Reed stood up and bowed. Then he sat down and

then stood up again, like he had just won a golden ticket. 'Thank you!' he whispered to Pop. 'Thank you!' he breathed shakily, gazing at Henry.

'Now,' said Pop, rubbing his hands with glee. 'Who would like to hear a joke?'

Reed snapped to attention. 'Me!'

'Well,' said Pop. 'I dreamt about drowning in an ocean made of fizzy drink last night—'

'Oooooh, no,' groaned Dylan.

'If it sounds like a grandad joke,' said Jay. 'And it smells like a grandad joke—'

'It took me a long while to work out it was just a Fanta sea.' Pop clicked his tongue. 'Get it?'

'Aaaa-aaaah!' Reed scratched his head.

Dylan slumped over. 'It *is* a grandad joke!'

'Ha,' said Reed. 'I get it now. Fanta sea as in *fantasy*.'

'You don't like that one, boys?' asked Pop. 'Don't worry, I've got more. What do you call an alligator wearing a vest?'

Jay grabbed his ears as if they were bleeding. 'Heeee-eeelp!' he cried.

'An investigator!' Pop slapped his knee.

Cassie giggled. She squeezed her Pop's hand. She glanced over at Henry, her eyes gleaming. Henry smiled back. He knew for some people, bad old grandad jokes told a million times over were the best kind of wish come true.

WELL and TRULY MADE

Henry wiped the sweat from his eyes. He stood puffing at the very top of the hill. He rested his bike against his hip and gazed down at the the main beach below, where lifeguards, tiny as specks, stared out over the surf.

Cassie flung her arm out, making a proper, formal introduction. 'This is Ballingally Tops. The steepest hill around here.' She bowed her head, as if the hill deserved solemn respect.

'Holy Polymoley!' breathed Henry. The lagoon at the back of the beach was so small and faraway, it looked like a poured-out cup of billy tea.

'There's no hill higher,' said Cassie. She tugged at the bike helmet strap beneath her chin. 'Except for Rumbler Mountain.'

No hill higher.

Henry cleared his throat. Sheezy-Louisy! Riding his bike down it would be insanity, like hurtling down a sharp, breathtaking slide straight out of a carnival show.

'Do you still want to ride down?' asked Cassie. She swivelled Blinter's front wheel from side to side.

'Well.' Henry wiggled his helmet. He scrunched up his nose. 'I don't know.' He peered up at a small cloud sailing past, so close he could almost touch it. 'Do you?'

'Hmmm,' said Cassie. 'Maybe. Or maybe not. You don't really notice how long and high it is when you're climbing up and looking down at your feet and pushing the bike and hoping your lungs won't explode and then you get to the top and you think…yeeeeek!'

Henry shivered. 'You can see everything from up here.'

'I know.'

Ribbons of silky blue water snaked in from the sea, weaving past the wharf and the holiday park, threading under the Yelonga Bridge.

'We could always walk back down and go out to Nugget Rock and say goodbye to Bluebell and Hazel and Buttercup and Daisy and grumpy-pants Myrtle one more time?'

It was the very last day.

They had tried so hard to fit everything in; snorkelling in the Hole, totem tennis, Sea Pony in the pool with Lulu and a game of Cheat under the tarp with Carey, Jay, Dylan and Patch, which Henry had won with grand, genius flair. They had jumped on the giant pillow and eaten double scoops of banoffee gelato for afternoon tea and spent a long time patting Heathcliff at the wharf, but Henry had a nagging sensation the whole time that his holiday would not be complete unless he rode Peg down at least one *hill of death.*

'Have you ridden down this hill before?' asked Henry.

'Only from halfway,' said Cassie. 'From near the cemetery. Where my Nan is.'

The cemetery. Oh, gosh, Henry didn't want to think about the cemetery, in the same way he didn't want to think about the fact his skull contained a brain. But if you were going to be silly enough to ride down a *hill of death*, a cemetery was one of the places you could possibly end up in. He knew that for a fact!

'Let me tell you, it's still pretty scary riding down, even from halfway.'

Holy Momoley! Was he waiting, again, for the exact right moment? Even though he had survived a ferocious storm on the first day of the holidays, as bad as a gigantic tornado? Even though he'd ventured out and rescued a lost pony in the middle of the night, even though he was petrified of the dark and dragons and werewolves and zombies and all of Lulu's scary concoctions?

Hadn't he learnt how to ride his bike, even though he was terrified? Even though he crashed into a prickly rosemary bush? Even though Reed had taunted him the whole time and he was so worried about what everyone might think? Hadn't he ridden his bike to Nugget Rock with his dad and sped down a small hill of death? Hadn't he said sorry to Cassie for not being straight-up and true? Hadn't he touched a fierce, wild animal like Heathcliff with his bare hands? Hadn't he felt the echo of that fierce, trembling wildness rise up in him too?

Wasn't he a genius at noticing funny moments like small treasure? And at playing board games and eating gelato and listening and making friends and trying hard? Couldn't he be good at making a tiny bit of room for the worry, without giving it the whole house?

Henry flicked the spikes on his helmet. He could do it. He wanted to do it. He knew he had the right sort of courage somewhere. He climbed on his bike. He launched out across the road, his legs shaky. The front wheel wobbled from side to side.

'I'm ready,' he whispered.

'Okay,' said Cassie, tightening the straps of her helmet.

The mothy flutter of worry was in Henry's chest. But something else too, a secret shimmer in his tummy, like a tiny bunch of glittery fish were waiting to leap towards the sun. He took a deep breath. He turned Peg's front wheel downwards, towards the wharf side of the hill.

'Wheeeeeee-heeeeeeeeeeeeeeeeeeee!' he screeched, as he lunged forward.

'Whoooooo-hooooooooooooooooo!' shrieked Cassie, dinging her bell.

The wind whistled in Henry's ears.

The cable ties tack-tacked. Cool air puffed from the dappled shade. Heat roared up from the road. Cassie's wheels purred close behind.

Henry swept down over the very first dip and he felt his tummy rise and float, like it might never come down again. When the bike landed with a smack, he laughed out loud, as if someone had tickled him. He loosened his shoulders, bent his elbows and relaxed his grip. He tucked himself into the bike, until he was tight and small.

He plunged down past the cemetery and the golf course, leaning into the curves. The world poured by in a blur of blue and green and bugs and birds. There were moments when Henry was certain he was skimming above the road, gliding like a grey-winged horse. He was sure the earth was turning in the opposite direction, right before his eyes.

Holy Smamoley!

His heart was hammering. Water was streaming from his eyes and down his cheeks. He wasn't crying, but maybe he could. But he wanted to laugh too, big, loud, gulping, rejoicing whoo-hoos of delight. He was exuberant, buoyant, afloat, as if nothing would ever sink him.

He knew what a bike meant now.

It was fun, adventure, danger, speed, balance, power and strength. It was wind and wings and freedom, the whole world blooming fresh, right before his eyes.

When Henry reached the bottom, he braked so hard he skidded to a stop in the rubbly shoulder of the road. Leaf litter flung up around him. 'Whoooaaaaaaaah!' he breathed.

'Heeeeeeeeee!' squealed Cassie, her brakes screeching, as she slithered into the corner. 'Haaa! *We made it!*'

They gazed at each other, red-faced and puffing. They were silent for a long moment. A magpie warbled a song in the tree above. Gum leaves twizzled down.

Henry grinned. 'Do you want to do that again?'

Cassie laughed. 'Race you to the top!'

Henry and Cassie rode slowly back to the holiday park. 'Holy Spamoley! My legs are jelly!' said Henry, with a snort.

Cassie giggled. 'Maybe six times down that hill was too much.' Her front wheel wobbled.

'Henry,' shouted Lulu. She dropped her skipping rope and danced down the bike path towards them. 'Henry! Guess what! GUESS WHAT! Reed caught five kingies, three albacore, seven bream, six tailors, two trevallies, eight flounders and four mullets. And he's saved the best and biggest kingie for you. And we are going to have a fish feast. And everyone's been invited, the WHOLE holiday park, as soon as Reed gets back from the hospital.' Her eyes were wide, her cheeks round and pink as plums.

'The hospital?' Henry braked. He balanced on one foot. 'Did he hurt himself?'

'No...no...no,' Lulu said. 'But he was very sick out on the boat.' She nodded at Cassie. 'Your Pop said he did an awful lot of vomiting. The most vomiting he has ever seen. But Reed didn't let that stop him because he was too busting to catch a kingie. And when the fish started biting, he didn't want to stop, even though his dad wanted him to.'

'Is he going to be okay?' asked Henry.

'Oh, yes! They're just taking him to the hospital as a...what do you call it... a pre...something—'

'Precaution?' suggested Cassie.

'Yes! That's right,' said Lulu. 'In case they need to dehydrate him!'

'Rehydrate, I think.' Cassie pressed a hand against her lips. She stole a quick glance at Henry. He swallowed back a smile.

'Yes, that's what I *said*,' exclaimed Lulu, shaking her head in annoyance. 'But he made me promise to tell you, Henry, that the big kingfish is just for you!'

'Woweee!' said Henry.

'And he was so happy, Henry,' said Lulu. 'Even though his face was green as a gherkin, he was smiling. Smiling so huge, it was like he found every single present on his Christmas list right underneath his tree.' Lulu hopped about on one foot. 'And Reed's dad said it was the most beautiful thing he's ever seen and that Reed's holiday has now been well and truly made!'

Well and truly made! Henry thought about those words for a second. A crisp, clear gladness crinkled right through him.

'And Henry,' interrupted Lulu, 'can I have a bite of your big kingie?'

Henry nodded. 'Sure thing, Lulu.'

Lulu skipped away. 'Super!' she sang. 'Super-dooper! Super-dooper-*pooper*!'

A HUGE,
HEAPED PLATE

Henry and Cassie cruised the tables spread out
with food.

'Crispy noodle salad,' said Henry, pointing at
a dish. 'Tick! My favourite. I'm going to have a big
scoop of that!'

Cassie slid further down. 'A beefy thing here.
With nuts!'

'Someone else can eat that.'

'It might be nice,' said Cassie.

'I don't think so.'

Cassie laughed. 'You never know.'

Fish were sizzling on a nearby barbecue. Pop and
Reed were standing side by side, wrapped in navy
aprons. They were click-clacking their tongs and
flapping their flippers like they were conductors.

'The maestros are at work,' said Dad to Henry, with a wink.

Crowds of people were gathered around, sniffing up the fresh deliciousness of lemon and salt and garlic and chilli. The nuggety rugrats from next door were listening eagerly to Pop's tales of Reed's daring adventure. 'Now let me tell you about how the lad reeled this one in! It was an epic Moby-Dick fight, I'm telling you,' cried Pop, pointing at the biggest fish on the barbecue.

Patch and Jay and Dylan lounged on the grass, near the water's edge, talking with the coconut girls.

Dad slid a salad bowl onto the table. 'Whoo-hooo! Here's another potluck dish! Corn and bacon and avocado, with a twist of lime. So I've been told.'

'Hmmm-mmm,' said Henry to Cassie. He licked his lips. 'Ba-con. I lo-ove bacon.'

'Would you look at this feast!' said Dad. 'So much bounty to share! I can't wait to taste them all.' He bent and scruffed Lulu's hair.

'Don't!' Lulu reached up and pressed her hair back down. She was sitting on the grass, surrounded by the big bikies. Each one held a pony on their lap, because Lulu was teaching them, in great detail, about the art of grooming. 'Their manes can be quite tricky,' she confided. 'And they get very fussy and snorty when you have to work through their knots. I find it helps if you sing to them very loudly. But not lullabies. They hate lullabies. But they LOVE love songs.'

Henry leant over another bowl and sniffed. 'Potato salad with egg and tiny green things. Yeulch!'

'This one is chicken caesar salad,' said Cassie. 'It's got the little bread cubes in it. They are so crunchy. Sometimes they have anchovies. Do you know what they are?'

Henry shook his head. 'Nope.'

'They're tiny little fish with the biggest ker-pow taste. My Nan loved them so much she could eat them all on their own, straight from the jar. I don't like them. They're too salty and oily and sluggy and— whoah!' Cassie pointed at a dish in the middle of the table. 'Who made that?'

'Who made what?' asked Henry. He stared at a basket containing a crusty buttered breadstick.

'That salad!' said Cassie, pointing at a cracked yellow bowl, edged with pink rosebuds.

'Are you sure that *is* a salad?' Henry stood on tiptoe to look closer. It looked nothing like a salad to him. There was not one iota of green in it, for a start. 'What are those white things?'

'Marshmallows,' said Cassie.

Henry screwed up his nose. 'And the orange stuff?'

'Mandarin,' said Cassie. 'Little segments of mandarin. And crushed pineapple and shredded coconut. All stirred in together with sour cream.'

'Sour cream!' said Henry. 'Holy Glamoley! That doesn't sound like a salad at all!'

'Where did it come from?' Cassie peered around the tents. 'Do you know?'

Henry tugged at the collar of his shirt. 'Nope,' he said. 'Anybody could have brought it.'

'Oh, my goodness!' Cassie rushed forward around the tables, across the grass. She gazed down the bike path as if she was searching for something. She turned and looked up the bike path.

'What's wrong?' asked Henry.

Cassie circled back. Her face was flushed and she was breathless, like she had run a long way. 'That salad...it was my Nan's favourite.' She trudged back across the grass, pinching her bottom lip. 'She always made it...on special occasions. And just for a second I—'

'Ah, gosh,' said Henry.

'I thought...but then...of course, you know.' Cassie's head drooped. Her neck was thin and pale as a stalk.

Henry gazed up at the sky, at the first wish star beginning to bloom. 'You know what?' He stood up straight. 'I'm going to eat a double helping of that salad.' He clenched his fingers tight. 'And I'm pretty sure it's going to be delicious. The nicest thing I've ever eaten. Even if it does have mandarin in it.'

Cassie sniffed, then laughed, her eyes glistening.

Henry crumpled the edges of the tablecloth. 'And anyway, who's to say your Nan wouldn't send you a marshmallow salad? Who's to say she wouldn't send you that, instead of a shooting star, so you can know she's still thinking of you even in heaven?'

'Oh, Henry,' whispered Cassie. 'Yes!' A smile broke out across her face.

Henry blushed, red as a can of crushed tomatoes. He opened his mouth to say something more, but just at that moment Reed rushed up, huffy and sweaty. He held out a platter like he was making an offering to royalty. 'Henry!' he said, almost bowing. 'The big kingie. It's ready. It's done. It's all yours. I hope you enjoy it.'

Henry gazed down at the fish. It was gigantic, staring up at him with a fevered, disapproving eye. Holy Dramoley! He wasn't sure he could eat it. He swallowed, trying to dislodge the big lump in his throat.

'I'm going to stay right here with you, to see you take your very first bite,' said Reed. 'I want to know what you think!'

Henry nodded. He took the proffered platter. A puff of soy and ginger stung his nose. He glanced at Reed's flushed, proud, anxious face.

It came to Henry then that perhaps true friends could be found in unexpected places. It struck him that sometimes a fish was more than just a fish. That sometimes a salad was more than just the bits and pieces that made it up. He knew in a flash that eating a huge, heaped plate of marshmallow salad with mandarin, topped with a barbecued kingfish with a bulging, mad eye was a big, wild way of saying yes to the grand, genius adventure of being a straight-up and true friend. And funnily enough, he wouldn't change a thing.

BEGINNINGS
and ENDINGS

On the morning they packed up, all the grown-ups were snappy and cranky. Even Dad was grumpy, his happy mood sunk like a tall ship. 'Would you hurry it up!' he growled at Patch, who was fiddling with the tarp ropes. 'We're not on teenage time now. We need to fold this tarp up, collapse the tent, pack the trailer, hitch it on and be out of this place by ten, so the next family can move in.'

Henry hated the idea of another family moving into their spot. He hated thinking about them setting up their tent and their tarp and their kitchen and camp chairs, riding their bikes on the bike path out front. He wanted to pretend that this site would be empty for the whole year, waiting for them to come back the very next summer.

The sun beat down like a hot hissing iron against the top of his head.

Every time Henry wanted to go and find Cassie, his mum found him another job. First he carried the clothing crates and pillows and bed rests to the trailer. Then he helped Lulu fold her sleeping bag. After they finished wrestling the slippery, rustling thing back in its bag, like some kind of crazy miracle, Henry was ordered to wash and dry the breakfast dishes. Later he followed Mum around the tent, while she swept every blade of grass and every speck of dirt into his dustpan.

'Why isn't Lulu helping more?' said Henry, groaning. His back and legs were aching from too much crouching.

'Don't you worry about Lulu,' said Mum. 'She's keeping Kale entertained and that's a harder job than sweeping, let me tell you! It's going to take all her powers of persuasion and every pony trick in her repertoire to keep Houdini from escaping.'

'Henry, just worry about yourself!' cried Dad, from outside the tent. 'I've already told you!'

Holy Scramoley! Henry could tell even breathing might get him into trouble today. Just one tiny whistle out of his nose and his dad might go ballistic.

'It's like a hot-air balloon in here.' Mum wiped her top lip. 'I'm about ready to ignite!'

'At least it's not raining, that's all I can say,'

grunted Dad, as he dragged the fly off the tent. 'Patch, would you get over here now and stop looking at that phone! If I catch you so much glancing at it again, it's gone for the whole trip home.'

'Someone woke up at the wrong end of the sleeping bag,' muttered Patch through the mesh window, rolling his eyes.

'When you've finished in there, Henry, I want you to move your bike and the scooters and skateboards over to the trailer,' called Dad.

'No one's to go back into the tent now,' said Mum. 'It's been swept clean and I don't want anyone clodhopping through it.'

Henry dragged the scooters and the skateboards, one by one, towards the trailer. He saved Peg for last. The water glittered. The sky arched above him, an impossibly dreamy blue, while the grass beside the bike path rolled away smooth and green as a Granny Smith apple. Everything was so fresh and clear, inviting him, almost tempting him to go for one last ride...no, summoning him to stay forever, making it as difficult as possible to say goodbye.

'Yoooo-hoooo!' said Pop, ambling towards them through the pine trees. 'We've brought some sustenance, otherwise known as morning tea.'

'Yummy!' cried Lulu, letting go of Kale's hand. 'Mango! My favourite.'

'And some iced tea,' said Mrs Barone. 'What a lifesaver!'

'And apple-blackberry juice!' shouted Lulu.

'Yum.' Kale poked his head through his legs.

'Thank you! Thank you! Thank you!' Mum rested her chin against her clasped hands, as if Pop and Cassie were an answer to prayer.

'And a pink tea bun,' said Cassie, grinning. '*Without* sultanas.'

'Whoo-hoo!' cried Patch. 'Morning tea time! Ding-a-ling-ting!'

Everyone emerged from behind their trailers and tents, wiping their sweaty faces and sighing with relief, eager to forget the racing clock. They drank iced tea and juice, munched on tea bun and sucked on the mango cheeks until they were bare, while everyone laughed and joked and told stories and teased and lived back on holiday time, just for a little while.

Henry and Cassie wandered down towards the water's edge. 'Everyone's been so mad today.' Henry licked the icing off the end of his bun.

Cassie wiped a crumb from her top lip. 'Well, my Nan always says being mad is just another way of being sad,' she said.

Henry stopped licking. 'Oh.' He chewed that thought over in his mind for a second. He hadn't thought of getting mad like that before. But maybe if you were a grown-up and you wanted a holiday to go on forever and ever, then the end of a holiday would be as horrible as a dark rain cloud shadowing your heart. Maybe if you were a grown-up, getting grumpy was a little bit easier than bawling your eyes out.

Cassie beckoned to Henry. 'I've got something to tell you,' she whispered.

Henry popped the last bite of his bun into his mouth and followed her down through the reeds, squelching through the mud and out onto the sandflats.

'So,' Cassie said, twisting the hem of her T-shirt. 'The thing is…my mum is coming home from a cruise at the end of February.'

'Oh wow!' said Henry, swallowing quickly. 'That's good.'

'I know,' said Cassie. 'On the *Gypsy Princess*.'

Henry dug a big toe into the sand. 'Well, maybe this time it will be forever. Maybe this time she'll have grown tired of singing and is going to come home for good.'

Cassie shrugged. 'I don't think so,' she said. 'But I'm still going to keep on wishing. But you know the other best thing?'

'No. What?'

'The *Gypsy Princess* is going to dock in Sydney and my Pop was thinking we could go up to meet her and that when we do, we could perhaps come by and visit you and your family too. And I will get to see you again and not so long away.' She smiled at him, her eyes shiny and exultant.

A dark rain cloud rose from around Henry's own heart. Ah, he got it now. He understood. Sometimes it was hard to know just exactly how low and sad you were until the feeling actually lifted.

Henry would get to see Cassie again and not so long away. She wouldn't be lost to him forever. Even though he was going home to Beatle and to Nonna and to Year Three and to his old friends and a new teacher. Even though his summer holiday was nearly done.

'Whoo-hooooo!' he shouted. And all of his loud, gulping, rejoicing delight spilt out like a flood. 'Whoooooooooooo-hooooooo!' He zoomed about the sandy shallows, his arms outstretched like a winged horse, skimming and gliding above the earth.

Cassie laughed and laughed. Then she leapt and stretched out her arms and the two of them ran, sweeping and swooping.

Henry would see Cassie again. Yes, he would. The best, grand genius friend he had ever met on his way to somewhere else. Because this wasn't an ending, but a beginning.

The wind whistled in the roof racks as the car sped along the highway towards home. Every now and again, the trailer jolted and jiggled.

'You locked it on okay?' said Henry.

'Yes, matey,' said Dad, looking at him in the rear-view mirror. 'I did. I triple quadruple checked it too.'

Lulu was fast asleep. Her head bobbed up and down and her hot bare foot rested on Henry's knee. A silvery strand of drool hung like a fishing line right down to her shoulder.

'Are you sure?' Henry itched around the scab on his shin.

'Absolutely.'

'I don't want it to fall off.'

'How much longer?' Lulu opened her bleary eyes for a second.

'Five and a half hours!' grinned Dad.

'Oh, no,' groaned Lulu, smooshing her hand across her mouth.

'Go back to sleep, sweetheart,' said Mum. 'It's a long while yet.'

'Okay,' sighed Lulu, licking her lips. She nestled back into her booster, hugging Clover tighter to her chest.

Henry patted Lulu's foot soothingly. 'But what if it did fall off?' He glanced over at Patch. He was leaning his head against the window, his eyes tightly shut, his earphones plugged in, his leg joggling away.

'Your bike couldn't get more secure, Heno. I promise you! Okay?'

'Okay. Good! Fine.'

Henry thought about Peg on the back of the trailer, gleaming like a silver moonbeam, the front wheel whizzing. He couldn't wait to show Nonna how he could ride. He couldn't wait until he could show Beatle. Maybe he could even take Beatle for a ride in the dog park. Or maybe he could even start to ride his bike to school on his own? Holy Vamoley! The last thing Henry wanted was for Peg to fall off the back of the trailer into some thicket of bush, never to be found again.

'You know what?' said Mum. 'It's so funny. When I left home to go on holidays, I felt a little pang of sadness. And now I'm leaving holidays to go home and there it is again, the same little pang. What do you make of that?'

'You know,' said Dad, planting a big kiss on the side of Mum's head, 'you are a mysterious and wonderful woman.'

Henry thought for a long moment. He pondered the warm comfort of home and Beatle and Nonna and his own squishy bed. And then he thought about his holiday and Cassie, playing cricket and cards, eating feasts with the other families, under a sky full of stars. He thought about the sound of the sea roaring at night, the smell of salt and hot bread and bacon in the morning, making wishes, licking creamy banoffee gelato and trying his first ever kingfish. He thought about Lulu and werewolves and rescuing Clover and Patch teaching him how to ride Peg, on his own. He thought about sadness and magic, and making a true friend and the surprising, unexpected discovery that sometimes a holiday could turn a person inside out like a pocket, into something new.

'Well...maybe all best good true things give you a pang when you leave them or they leave you,' he said slowly. 'Otherwise...maybe they wouldn't be best good true things?'

'Ah, Henry!' said Mum, breathing out a big sigh. 'Oh, yes! Of course. It makes sense when you say it like that.' She rustled around in the glove box. 'On that lovely note, who would like a lolly?'

'Not for me, thanks,' said Dad.

'Me, please,' said Henry.

Mum tossed a barley sugar over her shoulder. Henry caught it first go.

'Great catch, numpty!' grunted Patch, with his eyes closed.

'What?' said Henry. 'Hey! How did you know?'

Patch opened one eye. 'It's my sick extra-sensory perception!' He winked at Henry. 'So...how about when we get back home, I take you down to the BMX jumps by the duck pond?'

Henry felt a little flutter in his chest.

He imagined Peg flying up and over a giant jump. 'Ooooh, yeah,' he breathed.

Patch nodded. 'Awesome!'

Henry gazed out the window, at the hazy green wide world.

Holy Gramoley! It was a grand, genius summer. There were no other words for it.

ACKNOWLEDGEMENTS

A zillion billion thanks...

to Erica Wagner, Hilary Reynolds and the whole team at Allen & Unwin, for the endlessly good ways you have all made Henry so at home in the world,

to Judy Watson for your glorious illustrations, and Debra Billson for your gorgeous design,

to Barbara Mobbs, my agent, for the many tremendous years of straight-up and true wisdom,

to Miss Cole and her class for being such a kind and generous first audience,

to all the wonderful friends we've camped with over the years, but especially the Clement, Russell, Stelzer and Warren families, with deepest gratitude for so many grand, genius summers,

and to Keiran, Bryn, Riley and especially Rohan, who was Henry's champion from start to finish – bucketloads of love for all the laughs, long hugs and encouragement, and for all the bright, funny moments like small, quiet treasure.

ABOUT the AUTHOR

Lisa Shanahan is an award-winning writer of picture books and fiction for young people. Her first novel for teenagers, *My Big Birkett*, was published to critical acclaim both in Australia, where it was short-listed for the CBCA Book of the Year for Older Readers, and in the United States. Her picture book *Bear and Chook by the Sea*, illustrated by Emma Quay, was the CBCA Book of the Year for Early Childhood in 2010. Her picture book *Big Pet Day*, illustrated by Gus Gordon, was the Speech Pathology Book of the Year for Ages 5–8 in 2015.

Lisa loves moon-gazing, making up words, mango sorbet, mock orange blossom, black cockatoos, shouts of unexpected laughter, the weight of a scruffy dog resting on her knee and hot cups of tea. She lives in Sydney, close to the river of her childhood, with her husband and their three sons.